DOG
TOWN

Luīze Pastore lives on the outskirts of Riga and runs workshops and creative writing classes for children around Latvia. She won the Latvian Literature Award for the Best Children's Book of 2013 with **Dog Town** (*The Tale of the Maskatchka District*) which is also being made into an animated feature film – *Jacob, Mimi and the Talking Dogs*. Luīze has also received several awards for her *Art Detectives* series including the White Ravens 2016, Pastariņš Prize 2017, International Baltic Sea Region Jānis Baltvilks Prize in Children's Literature and Book Art 2015, Latvian Children's Jury Award 2016 and The Latvian Literature Prize for The Best Children's Book 2016.

DOG TOWN

by Luīze Pastore

Illustrations by Reinis Pētersons

Translated by
Žanete Vēvere Pasqualini

Firefly

This English edition first published in 2018 by Firefly Press
25 Gabalfa Road, Llandaff North, Cardiff, CF14 2JJ
www.fireflypress.co.uk

Originally published in Latvian as *Maskačkas stāsts*
(The Tale of the Maskatchka District)
Text © Luīze Pastore 2013
Illustrations © Reinis Pētersons 2013
Translation © Žanete Vēvere Pasqualini 2018

Published in English by arrangement with Neputns Ltd, Latvia
www.neputns.lv

Neputns

A CIP catalogue record of this book is
available from the British Library.

Print ISBN 978-1-910080-72-6
Typeset by: Elaine Sharples
Printed by Pulsio SARL
Supported by

Latvijas Rakstnieku savienība

Latvija 100 ≣

Kultūras ministrija

Contents

Riga is ready   1

A ship on Brīvības Street   7

Disaster   17

Punishment for drowning Riga at the
bottom of the Daugava River   24

Mimi, Eagle and the golden tooth   34

The Boss of Maskatchka   49

Jacob, the bird of misfortune   62

Searching for the former shadow   72

The duck who didn't have time to
feel unhappy   88

Skyscraper Forest   101

For a free Maskatchka   113

Conman Skyscraper, a spy and his
bodyguard   124

All the wishes in the world   137

A specially protected breed of dog   150

The tiny skyscraper   164

High time for the bird of misfortune
to feel happy   178

The myth of Riga

Riga, where this story is set, is the capital of Latvia, one of three countries on the southern edge of the Baltic Sea, between Poland and Russia.

Like all countries, Latvia has many legends. One of them is the *Myth of Riga*. The myth says that work to build Riga can never be completely finished because then it would be drowned in the Daugava River which runs through the middle of the city, and the building work would have to start all over again.

Once every hundred years a water spirit rises from the Daugava and asks the first person it meets whether the city is ready. If that person says yes, Riga, with all its residents, will sink under the water. But as everyone living in the city knows this legend, they always answer the spirit that Riga is not ready, so to this day Riga is still standing.

Riga is ready

What Jacob wanted most of all was for an enormous one-eyed comet to crash down onto the city. Or failing that, some other massive disaster that would make the dark, catfish-filled waters of the river Daugava overflow their banks and swirl through the streets and avenues of Riga. Then fabulously tall ships as high as nine-storey buildings would glide proudly along Brīvības Street, right past Jacob's dining-room window, carrying highly valuable secret cargoes to warmer, distant shores.

The night before, Jacob had screwed up all his courage and, his voice trembling, whispered:

'Riga is READY!'

Now, waiting for the evening news at half past eight, butterflies were fluttering madly in his stomach. He hoped with all his heart to hear shocking news about Riga sinking to the bottom of the Daugava River, or some other natural catastrophe that would transform the familiar view from his dining-room window into something wonderfully different.

If the disaster came, he thought he would be absolutely the best person to help the ships' captains – he knew the city streets like the back of his hand, even though he hardly ever got to walk down any of them. Children were strictly forbidden to go out on the streets of Riga by themselves. But how could you have fun with grown-ups watching?

Children were forbidden from doing virtually everything here: talking to strangers; getting into cars; crossing the street at a red light, even if there were no cars around. They were not allowed to play ball on the pavement or in the courtyards – especially if it was washday and those white linen sheets that you were told never to touch, were drying in the sun under watchful eyes hidden in the ground-floor apartments.

But all these rules were pointless if children were not even allowed out on the streets on their own! It made more sense just to stay at home.

Jacob was allowed out with his dad … but his dad was always at work. So Jacob watched the world go by from his dining-room window and he knew everything he saw off by heart. At home on his own, he spent days on end stretched out on the windowsill, watching the noisy comings and goings on the main street below.

Actually children weren't allowed to stay at home on their own either, but that was harder to check up on because they also weren't allowed to open the door to strangers.

When Dad came home from work he would often say, "Give me a moment to myself, I need some grown-up time, please!"

There was clearly some subtle connection between being a grown-up and being on your own, in which case Jacob had already been a grown-up for quite a while. In fact ever since his tutor, Mademoiselle Poupette, had stopped coming and, shortly afterwards, Marta the housekeeper had disappeared too. She must have decided to devote herself full-time to keeping her own home tidy, or maybe the home of that man she used to mention so often – Jesus Christ.

Jacob's mum was not there. Jacob knew that some children only have their dads with them. Others only have a mum. These things happen.

Jacob's dad worked long hours, spending most of his time being a big, important boss and not a dad. But at weekends when the two of them, Jacob and Peter Bird, went on expeditions to the city-centre department stores, they sometimes threw in a few extra rounds of the streets of Riga. On these days, Jacob swapped his usual view from the dining-room window for the deafening noise of the city's main road – Brīvības Street – with its wafts of food and courtyard smells, exhaust fumes, maddening commotion and noisy conversations. Grand buildings literally sprang up before Jacob's eyes and transformed themselves into a huge living, breathing city. His eyes grew as wide as satellite dishes, trying to take it all in. His ears opened wider to hear everything better. Amazed birds could easily have found themselves inside Jacob Bird's wide-open mouth, having mistaken it for the opening of a nest box. He was too young to be allowed a phone, but he made sure that he memorised everything, down to the last detail, so that he could mark it all down back home on his handdrawn *Map of the Ships of Riga*.

A ship on Brīvības Street

The summer was so hot that Jacob had no problem imagining the terrible, one-eyed comet taking the sun's place above the city, curling up innocently like a cat and nervously twitching the burning tip of its tail, just waiting for the right moment to strike and cause an earth-shattering disaster.

Jacob was alone at home. Again. Sometimes he could hear dull noises and echoes from the courtyard thudding through the open kitchen window behind him into the otherwise silent, four-roomed flat. Once in a while, pigeons landed on the tin windowsill and strutted about, always as curious as the first time they appeared there. They'd fly away again,

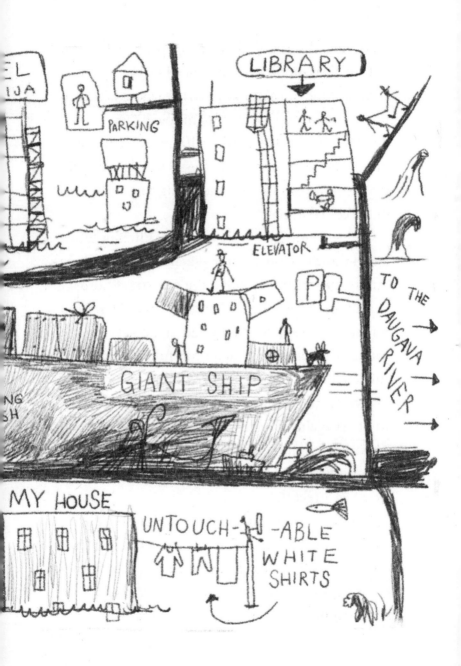

their wings thwacking like a newspaper being shaken out. In the complete silence he thought he could even hear the sun gliding across the wooden kitchen floor, climbing up his spine to his neck then leaping up between the slats of the half-empty shelves and drying the spots of water on the sink ... late at night the furniture too could be heard sighing with relief in the cool darkness.

Today, leaning eagerly over the kitchen table, Jacob was drawing a ship navigator's map, to help sailors find their way along the city street fjords.

Suddenly, between Elizabetes and Dzirnavu Street, progress was stopped abruptly by the sound of ships' horns. Jacob carefully scanned the side streets on the map where some unfortunate, lost vessel might have gone off course. The horns went off again. Where were the ships? And again! Then Jacob remembered where he was and went to squint through the spyhole in the door of his Brīvības Street flat.

'I know you're at home – open the door!' called the commanding voice of a strange creature with a huge head and a bony bulk of a body (they all looked the same through the spyhole) pressing on the doorbell again.

'I can hear you BREATHING there, behind the door,' the creature commented crossly, after waiting a while.

Jacob jumped back from the door.

'There's no one here, just me!' he called back.

'Oh, Jacob!' the tone of the voice changed. 'It's me, Mrs Schmidt. Do you remember me? I'm the landlady!' she purred from the other side of the door and pressed her head up close to the spyhole, her nose broadening like a giant cucumber.

'Open the door,' she pleaded.

When Jacob finally did open the door the woman seemed to fill the entire entrance hall with her small head and large body. 'It's not polite to keep a lady waiting,' she remarked. 'Go and tell your dad I'm here, would you?'

Jacob suddenly realised what he had done. He had opened the door to a stranger when he was *all alone* at home! He was going to be in real trouble.

'Run along, now.'

Mrs Schmidt was talking particularly loudly and slowly, as if children couldn't hear or understand properly, just because they were shorter and the words had to travel further to their ears. 'What's the matter? Are you feeling unwell? You look really pale. You don't get much sun, do you? Let me feel – your forehead is burning up! You must be really ill!'

An idea popped into Jacob's head. He arranged his face into a grimace of pain and whimpered, 'It's my heart, it hurts … Dad's run down to the chemist to get some medicine. He'll be back any second.'

Mrs Schmidt clapped her hands, thinking, *The poor boy, he's really sick, and here am I, coming at such a bad time with the unpaid bills. Just look at him, he needs to go straight back to bed!*

Meanwhile Jacob was shifting nervously from one foot to the other, worrying about how the ship was doing all on its own on Brīvības Street without him to guide it.

'Is it really sore?'

Jacob nodded a bit too quickly to be totally believable so, just to be on the safe side, he put his hand to his chest round about the spot where the ache was meant to be.

A shadow flitted across Mrs Schmidt's face. She narrowed her eyes and drew in her breath in disgust.

'It's very naughty to tell lies,' she finally spat out.

The entrance hall, and Mrs Schmidt with it,

suddenly started expanding, growing monstrously huge and Jacob, tiny as he already was, shrank even smaller – though sadly not small enough to be able to hide under the rug.

Mrs Schmidt was wagging a large, reprimanding finger in front of his nose.

'The heart is on the other side of the chest, boy! *On the left side*!'

She had grown quite angry.

'Every child knows which side the heart is on!'

It was like a sermon. 'If you go on lying like this, your heart really will get sick!'

Jacob gulped. It was all so horrible. And Mrs Schmidt showed no sign of calming down.

'Your father must have told you to give me this nonsense to try and get sympathy and pity from my marvellously generous, kind and noble heart. Is that it? But rest assured, he won't get out of paying all the rent he owes me that easily. I'll talk to him about this later!'

Mrs Schmidt turned on her heel and staggered up the stairs, still mumbling something about the recession, bills outstanding for months and also about the world coming to an inevitable end because, in her day, such horrid things really didn't happen.

Gradually the entrance hall went back to its original size. Jacob looked out of the window to make sure the terrible one-eyed comet was not approaching after all and the world was not actually coming to an end. Then he started wondering what his dad would say about him opening the door to a stranger.

'Every child knows that, bla bla bla...' The more Jacob thought about it, the more annoyed he became with that silly Mrs Schmidt who didn't seem to realise that he hadn't been a child for quite some time.

'And ... if I am not a child, I might very well not know exactly where the heart is!' Jacob muttered. 'Who on earth thought of placing the heart on the left side anyway? The right side is better. If my left leg itches, I always scratch my right leg too, even if it isn't itching, so it's not annoyed that I'm paying too much attention to the other one. OK, well ... hmph! So, it's on the left ... the heart is on the left...'

How on earth could the heart be on the wrong side?!

Jacob had often heard women in the courtyard talking about someone going over to the wrong side. Maybe this was some horrible, even incurable, heart disease, Jacob thought to himself as his Brīvības Street ship disappeared over the horizon.

Disaster

Jacob felt a long arm catch him, dragging him like a kitten away from the yawning darkness and into a wonderful ocean of light. But the journey was hard going as the wind hit him full force.

His fingers and toes felt like balloons, filled with air for the first time. He breathed in slowly and, as he did so, he realised he was back behind the kitchen table in the four-room apartment on Brīvības Street.

Reluctantly he opened his eyes. Where had he been? He must have been asleep, dreaming. Maybe the dream-man had noticed that Jacob

was about to wake up and had rushed to get him back into his body in time.

Jacob realised he was covered in goosebumps and shivering. A tremendous clap of thunder exploded just outside the window and he was shocked to find that he was soaked to the skin. Grey rain was streaming through the open kitchen window – as if someone outside was throwing in buckets of water.

The Brīvības Street that Jacob had drawn was all soaked with cuttlefish stains.

A key turned in the front door and Jacob's dad rushed into the kitchen, soaked through. The front door slammed loudly in the draught.

'Everything all right?' his dad asked, closing the kitchen window and dashing to get some towels from the bathroom.

Jacob said nothing. Jacob always found himself floating inside a big, shiny bubble when he first woke up and nothing from outside could reach him.

'Come here, Jacob!' Dad called out from the dining room. 'Come and look at the street, it's a real sight!'

Jacob joined his dad at the dining-room

window. It was hard to see anything through the torrential downpour. Then – puff – Jacob's bubble suddenly burst.

'Dad,' he said. 'THE DAUGAVA RIVER HAS INVADED THE CITY!'

Grey water swirled below them, greedily swallowing up Brīvības Street. Bewildered people stood at the crossroads as water surged around their waists; some clutched broken umbrellas while others clung to the traffic lights, hoping not to be swept off their feet. Others had climbed onto the roofs of water-logged cars. It was a terrifying sight – Brīvības Street looked like the deck of a huge, sinking ship caught in a mighty storm. This was not what Jacob had wished for! What had happened to the calmly flowing Daugava waters and graceful ships? And the townspeople? What would happen when the water rose above their heads?! When he had let his imagination run wild, he had forgotten all about them. Jacob started crying.

'Don't worry!' his dad said, comfortingly. 'We're on the fifth floor. Nothing will happen to us! Although it looks like our car is a goner...' He pointed as their car vanished below the waters.

'This isn't what I wanted, Dad!'

His father frowned. He paused for thought, water dripping into his eyes from his hair, then said, 'Right. We need to have a little chat. I spoke to Mrs Schmidt.'

Jacob didn't understand how Mrs Schmidt had anything to do with him flooding Riga with every last drop of water from the Daugava.

'I was most upset by what she told me, Jacob! Fancy saying you are seriously ill when you're perfectly healthy. That's lying!'

Now this too. Dad didn't understand a thing. Jacob tried to explain but his words came out in a jumble, his tears as uncontrollable as the rain outside the window. He had never wanted his dad to get into trouble but Mrs Schmidt had insisted

21

that he open the door. Besides, Jacob's immense, wonderful ship on Brīvības Street had been waiting for him. And the terrifying comet with its single, all-seeing eye had observed him and the disaster was never meant to be so bad – it should all have been quite low-key, no harm done at all. As his father waited for some sort of explanation, Jacob eventually blurted out:

'I … I said that Riga was READY!' Jacob finally owned up and, overcome with embarrassment, ran to bury his head in the sofa cushions.

To his immense surprise Dad snorted with laughter, which made things even worse. Dad didn't believe him! But there were those who did believe – those who knew only too well that it only took someone to say, without thinking, that Riga was finally ready, all the endless building work finally finished, and the city would be drowned for ever beneath the Daugava River.

Jacob felt incredibly lonely. Alone in the world, alone with a disaster that was all his fault.

His dad was still laughing.

He only stopped when he seemed to remember something. He sighed and looked quite serious. Then he picked Jacob up, even though he was quite grown up, and carried him to the bathroom, ran a hot tub of water for his son and sat down beside the bath. His dad's eyes kept wandering upwards to the ceiling. Occasionally he would open his mouth as if to say something and Jacob would freeze in horror, waiting for his punishment for having drowned Riga at the bottom of the Daugava River. But his dad would stop himself and the two of them just went on,

and on,

and on,

sitting there in silence.

Punishment for drowning Riga at the bottom of the Daugava River

Jacob had a restless night. A full yellow moon shone in through his window, or maybe it was the dangerous, one-eyed comet wearing a night shirt. Now the dream-man was on the alert and ready to transport Jacob both ways – from his bed in his fifth-floor bedroom of their four-room Brīvības Street apartment, to the world of dreams and back again.

Jacob found himself in a sunny apple orchard. And he wasn't alone – he knew his dad was there too, although the blinding sun cutting through the thick green leaves of the apple trees meant Jacob couldn't see him. The harder he looked for his dad, the brighter the sunlight became until Jacob couldn't see a thing, just the apple trees like immense, blindingly white rocks, encircling and protecting him.

Someone else was there, too. Someone Jacob couldn't see because they were always behind him. Every time Jacob turned round to try to catch a glimpse of whoever it was, they managed to hide quickly behind his back. It wasn't very nice. The harder he tried to see his dad, the more he was blinded by the sun and the more that *other* person behind his back stared at him.

Jacob started to run, only to find that the *other person* followed right behind him. Realising there was no point running, he stopped abruptly and, bending down as low as he could, looked between his own legs. He could see ... it was his shadow! Its eyes were immensely large and sad. For a moment, they just looked at each other, upside down, then the shadow turned a brisk somersault and got tangled up in Jacob's legs. Jacob tumbled, falling with a painful thud out of bed.

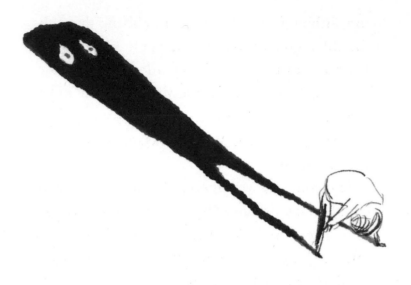

Blinded by the early morning sunlight, he leapt up and looked behind him – his grey shadow lay stretched out on the wooden floor like a well-behaved pet. He must tell his dad how his shadow had thrown him out of bed!

A delicious smell was coming from the kitchen. Pancakes and jam! The longed-for weekend was finally here.

When he'd eaten all his pancakes and was sure it was a good morning, Jacob smiled at his dad. At least he hadn't received his punishment for drowning Riga yet.

'Get dressed, we're going out,' his dad said.

Jacob would have jumped for joy if he hadn't still been a bit worried about getting into trouble. He asked his dad if they were going to board a ship to get out of the apartment.

Dad laughed and said that the city had gone back to being on dry land. Jacob ran to the window to see for himself and, sure enough, the view from the living-room window revealed a dirty street with broken street signs, a scattering of lost number plates and smashed umbrellas littering the pavement. It had gone back to being an ordinary street – quite dry. Secretly Jacob felt slightly disappointed – it all seemed *almost* back to normal. If only the threat of some awful punishment wasn't hanging over the city, and Jacob's head, all because he'd said *those* words.

'We're not going on any old outing,' his dad told him. 'I'm taking you to meet some of your relatives on the other side of town. You won't remember them – and I haven't seen them for years – but I'll show you where you'll be spending the summer. You'll get to know them better and have a great time together over the holidays. It'll do you good to spend time with other children.'

Suddenly Jacob felt a huge cloud was looming over the city, ready to burst at any moment and pour down rain over his head in fury.

'But … but … I really don't want to stay with these relatives and meet other children. I want to be with you.'

Dad coughed and repeated that Jacob would absolutely love it there. He would be able to go for walks every day.

'Will I?'

'Of course! And I'll come to visit at weekends. You can't stay on your own all the time anymore.'

Somewhere, out on the outskirts of Riga, there was a clap of thunder.

So was THIS to be his punishment for drowning Riga at the bottom of the Daugava River? His dad was going to stop loving him?

'Dad, I will *never* open our front door to anyone, ever again! I swear I won't, on the *tail of the comet*! Just don't be angry with me, please!'

Sighing heavily, his dad leaned back on the kitchen chair. He covered his face with his hands in silence. After a bit he said quietly, his voice catching,

'Jakey, it's not that simple. We are in quite a lot of trouble. You might not be able to understand that for now but, believe me, it's the only way.'

Dad turned away and didn't say anymore. His shoulders trembled very slightly.

Jacob knew that when his dad fell silent like this he had no chance of getting him to change his mind. There was no way to reach him and any attempt would only make him angry. The silent treatment was the worst thing of all – Jacob would much rather his dad had shouted and yelled at him. Feeling guilty, Jacob decided not to upset him further.

Maybe Dad would change his mind.

As good as gold, Jacob got dressed and brushed his teeth carefully – not just at the front but the back as well. He even combed his hair. A moment later his dad appeared behind him in the bathroom mirror, his large hand ruffling his neatly combed hair.

'You and me, we make a great team. Jake and Pete. Always the two of us, you and me! But it would do you good to make some new friends. You've never really had any and the thought scares you. I promise you'll have the best summer ever –

you won't even notice I'm not always there. And, if you do get a bit sad, trust me – we'll be together again soon enough. And you need to try to be sensible! When you wish for something, think it through first so things don't end up like they did yesterday. Even nasty wishes have a way of coming true, although not exactly in the way you intended.

'You know, if people don't make it clear how they feel and what they want, someone else might fill in the gaps, maybe adding their own ideas too – and that leads to misunderstandings and arguments.'

This all made perfect sense to Jacob.

'Just like you and me. In our own way we wished for something to change and, more likely than not, we didn't make ourselves clear and now everything has been turned upside down.'

When his dad left the bathroom, Jacob stared at the ceiling and whispered, 'We didn't wish for this to happen.'

Thinking it over, he added, 'Next time, I will make sure it's a smaller, less disastrous disaster…'

In answer a tiny, almost microscopic speck of white plaster fell from the ceiling and landed on the bathroom shelf among other particles of dust.

Mimi, Eagle and the golden tooth

Dad didn't change his mind.

The two Birds, Jake and Pete, crossed the entire city, and at long last Jake got to see lots of things. They went past the House of Philosophers (H.PH), where people think a lot and do very little, and the House of Grey Men (H.GM), where people don't think at all and do nothing, the Observatory, several Houses where People Lived Together Each Speaking Their Own Language (H.P.L.T.E.S.O.L) and other tall houses. Afterwards, Jacob made a careful drawing of all that he'd seen (without ships!)

They walked through a noisy, bustling marketplace, and Jacob noticed that the further they walked from the city centre, the lower the buildings became, and the streets were narrower and less crowded. Here were low wooden houses with lopsided verandas and gardens full of apple trees, hemmed in with old fences blackened with rot and bulging like large ladies' tummies. As he looked at the orchards, Jacob suddenly remembered last night's dream. He turned and checked behind himself – there was his shadow, glued to his heels, sneaking along the pavement like a black viper. A small wish in the form of a tear escaped from the corner of his eye. He wished that shadow would leave him alone! Jacob grasped his dad's hand even tighter. Sparrows splashed noisily in great big puddles which would later turn to ugly splats of mud in the heat of the sun.

They came out from under a bridge, and found a dull, grey, high-rise building right in front of them. One of its walls was decorated with a mural showing a strange, curvy creature holding some kind of sign in its hand.

'Ma … ma … ska … tchka …'

Maskatchka?!

Jacob didn't like the sound of the word at all. His dad told him it was the name of this part of the city. The district's real name was the Moscow Outskirts, which seemed even uglier, although there was nothing pretty about the district anyway with its crooked houses, dilapidated fences and the grey silence filling the gaps.

Out of nowhere, a large pack of dogs appeared and circled Jacob and his dad. The Maskatchka dogs followed the Birds in the direction of the big wooden house, sniffing the air around them mistrustfully.

Up until the very last moment Jacob had clung to the hope that his dad would change his mind or, better still, this would all turn out to be some sort of horrible misunderstanding.

The door of the ground-floor apartment opened to reveal a girl about two or three years older than Jacob. 'What do you want,' she asked, without answering his dad's greetings. She peered round the door at Jacob as he hid behind his father's legs.

'Oh, you must be looking for my dad, right?' she said, looking disappointed.

Jacob's dad said he was.

'I really don't know if I should let you in,' she added staring at Jacob rudely, looking him up and down from head to toe.

'Oh, is that so?! Why not?'

Seeing that Jacob's dad was trying not to laugh, the girl didn't bother replying.

Jacob's dad made the introductions. 'This is Jacob. Your dad is Jacob's mum's brother.'

'Oh really?! And where is Jacob's mum, may I ask?' the girl answered, still more rudely.

Surprised, Dad looked the horrible girl in the eye and said politely, 'As far as I am aware, she is not here.'

'No, she isn't,' the girl confirmed. 'There's no

mums here at all. There's only Eagle,' she added, before spinning round and disappearing into the dark apartment.

'EAGLE?' Jacob gasped.

'No, I haven't brought you to a wildlife park,' his dad whispered in his ear. 'Eagle, as your new friend called him, is your Uncle Ojārs. It's just his nickname.'

Jacob, feeling more and more upset, replied quietly, 'She's not my friend.' But his dad was already heading indoors where, a moment later, loud male voices could be heard. Jacob felt safer where he was and stayed in the entrance hall.

Lacelike fingers of mould grew in the corners of the hall. The place smelled of dill and damp earth.

Jacob had forgotten about the girl standing in the dark until she asked, 'How long are you going to stand there for?'

'What's your name?'

'Mimi,' she replied.

'That's not a proper name!'

'Yes it is! It means "Maria"!' the girl snapped back proudly. 'What about your name? Does it mean anything?'

Jacob didn't know that names were supposed to mean something. He felt deeply unhappy that Mimi had a name that meant something but he was just Jacob.

But it was Jacob's name they heard being called from the kitchen.

'And for your information, you're not my friend, either,' Mimi added before going to the kitchen.

'Jacob, come and say hello to your Uncle Ojārs!' his dad said.

The kitchen was warm and bright – a log stove was burning away even though it was summer. Jacob saw his uncle leaning against the windowsill smoking. Rings of smoke whirled above his clean-shaven head. He wore pale trousers rolled up to the knee and pulled in at the waist with a thick rope. Against them, his bare chest, muscly arms and deeply tanned wide shoulders stood out in contrast. His uncle was a strong man. He stared at Jacob with piercing, flinty eyes.

'Call me Eagle. That's what they all called me when I was a sailor. What do *you* want to be when you grow up? Mimi here wants to be a princess.' Jacob's uncle winked at him.

'No I do not!' Mimi protested, outraged. 'Princesses are all so *silly*!'

Jacob didn't think princesses were silly. In some of the old fairy tales, princesses got saved by heroes, didn't they? If there weren't any princesses, there would be no point to the story. Jacob shrugged.

If he had to be something, he would be a planner, he said bravely.

'What will you plan – affairs of state?' Eagle asked.

Jacob didn't know anything about affairs of state. He wanted to be the sort of planner who drew the city maps!

The grown-ups had coffee, the children sugary lemonade. Eagle talked a lot and Mimi disagreed with almost everything he said. The two Birds sat quietly on the narrow kitchen stools like sparrows on telephone wires; Dad listening and Jacob glancing furtively at the weird girl. Mimi didn't actually look much different from other girls but

Jacob's eyes were drawn to her; she was constantly wriggling like a small snake. Her face was round and freckled. She had a mane of dishevelled blonde hair, old chipped nail varnish of an indiscernible colour, and over her dark skinny jeans she wore a t-shirt with a faded picture of Pippi Longstocking holding a horse high above her head. He later found out that Eagle had brought it back for her from Sweden when he came back from one of his mysterious sea voyages. Miss Freckle had nailed the look completely – at that moment her nail-like look seemed to be boring a hole into Jacob's forehead.

Dad glanced at his watch.

Eagle caught him doing so and turned to Jacob. 'Yes, right. Your dad has work to do. The sooner he gets going, the sooner he will be back!'

Dad nodded in relief. Mimi frowned, obviously trying to work out what was going on. Jacob remembered why he was there. It was all so awful, Mimi was awful, and his dad didn't love him!

Mimi choked on her lemonade and, still spluttering, stared at Jacob. By the look on his dad's face, Jacob realised he'd spoken out loud.

'Do you want to hear about the time I faced

pirates on the high seas?' Eagle asked Jacob and Mimi groaned.

'There are *no* pirates. Just like there is no Father Christmas. I hope you are old enough to know that,' she said raising her eybrows.

The grown-ups shook hands. Dad turned to Jacob and, nervously clearing his throat, said: 'Be a good boy now. Don't let me down.'

And he left.

Every thought running through Jacob's mind grew quieter and quieter until they became soundless – the silence drilling into his eardrums, time slowed down and even the smallest movement required enormous effort.

Somewhere in the background a massive argument was going on. Mimi was shrilly insisting that she knew Father Christmas couldn't possibly exist as she had never seen him.

Eagle pointed out that as she had never been to the North Pole to check, she had no way of knowing that for a fact.

Mimi said that she believed in other things she had never checked up on herself, that the earth was round for example, which at least made some sense, unlike Father Christmas.

Eagle wondered whether, if there was a child in, say, faraway China who had never met Mimi and knew nothing about her life on the other side of the world in Maskatchka, it meant that Mimi didn't actually exist either.

Mimi said nothing, pouting defiantly as she looked out of the window.

'So Jacob, last winter I was at sea, on board an enormous ship carrying some very important, top-secret cargo to somewhere in Africa. I can't say where exactly as that's classified information,' Eagle began. In spite of himself Jacob started to listen. It was as if Eagle was sprinkling magic.

'After a week's sailing we eventually anchored off the African coast where we had to wait for a permit to unload the cargo. We couldn't go ashore without it and ended up not being allowed off the ship for a week – we spent day after day roasting under the African sun just waiting for a sign.

One night I woke up with the peculiar feeling that I wasn't alone in my cabin. I stared into the darkness trying to make out who or what was there (it was my sharp eyesight which earned me the nickname Eagle when I was at sea). And suddenly, there, in the pitch-dark cabin, I made out the glint of two restless eyes – nothing more! I realised what must have happened – under the cover of darkness pirates had crept on board and were quietly making off with what they thought were our most precious items of cargo. I had heard of this happening many times. Only those clever pirates had no idea that the most valuable thing on board, the very important, top-secret cargo, was in fact so secret that if you looked at it you would never imagine it was anything out of the ordinary! Those poor pirates were fooled just like anyone else.

Suddenly I heard the sound of fighting on the upper deck and shouts from other cabins. The eyes started twitching uneasily, maybe their owner had found nothing worth stealing in my cabin and was getting annoyed. A clink of metal told me that the pirate had unsheathed his dagger. I was sure he was coming for me so, hoping that my eyesight was better than his, I leapt out of my bunk at just the right moment and sunk my teeth in where I thought his neck would be with all my strength. My teeth were the only weapon I had, so thank goodness I still had my own and not false ones!' Eagle laughed heartily. 'Then I made a run for it. My eyesight might have been better than his but that pirate was much quicker on his feet than me; he was as nifty as a snake in the dark! He grabbed me in the doorway and stabbed me in the leg. As I lay on the floor, writhing in agony, he grabbed my gold wristwatch, tore the gold cross and chain from my neck and wrenched a tooth from my mouth!'

At this point, Jacob stopped believing Eagle's story. Why would a pirate steal a tooth? He could understand an elephant's tusk, but a tooth?

'Ah-hah.' Eagle opened his mouth wide and pointed to the gap in the front. 'That's where my

gold tooth was until it was cruelly yanked from my mouth!' Jacob's uncle moaned before giving a great belly laugh.

'The ship's boy told me later that none of them looked like the pirates in films – no eye-patches, wooden legs or hooks! No, no! They were just youngsters, not much older than you! You never know, maybe my gold tooth allowed a family to lead a golden life somewhere in Africa – and they all lived happily ever after.'

Jacob closed his mouth. He had *almost* forgotten how unhappy he was.

'What a load of nonsense,' Mimi snarled, although she'd listened eagerly to her dad's pirate story. 'Anyway, I'm off now. Things are happening in Maskatchka.' She jumped brusquely off her stool and headed for the kitchen door.

'Maybe you could invite Jacob along. Show him what's going on?' Eagle suggested.

'How about you taking him along to meet those pirates of yours? We only agreed to him staying here, not to me having to babysit all summer! I can't anyway, I've got too much to do,' she said and left the apartment, making sure she slammed the door behind her.

The Boss of Maskatchka

Jacob was at home on his own. He had already unpacked his stuff, and there wasn't much to do in the house. There wasn't much to look at from the ground-floor window either. The expressionless grey high-rise building with the strange mural on its side loomed just outside. A little to the right was a lonely tram stop without a bench, a pavement-lined street leading further into Maskatchka, and tram rails lying deep under layers of mud and grime. But over on the left (the side where the heart is) the dogs of Maskatchka were lying on a shady patch of grass under a group of trees. Every so often they raised their heads as half-empty, tired trams rumbled past, following them with their doggy eyes.

Once in a while Jacob saw Mimi go past. Eagle had assured him that Maskatchka was the safest place in the world. It was perfectly fine for children to go out on their own, he said. Just to be on the safe side though, for now, Jacob preferred to watch the goings-on from the window. But every time he saw Mimi walking past on her own he felt more confident about going out without a grown-up.

Eagle had said he would not be back until dinnertime, which was still a long way off. Mimi and Eagle were both very independent, returning from their separate explorations just before it got dark, meaning that dinner was at nightfall. Because it was summer that might be as late as 11pm. People ate at that time in Italy – Eagle the sailor had seen it himself. Jacob had heard that there were families with small children in Riga who ate at 6pm or 7pm, but Jacob and his dad and most of the other people he knew just ate whenever they were hungry. And Jacob was hungry now. He had to find something to do to forget about food, so he went out.

Mimi was nowhere to be seen. In fact, Jacob couldn't see a soul out there. There were no strangers to talk to, no cars to get into, no traffic lights flashing an angry red eye, no one to play ball with on washing day. Of course it was safe out there!

The dogs started barking and reminded Jacob that at least *they* were there. Their woofs became louder and louder. And angrier. They were barking at something in the distance, something too far off for Jacob to see. Then he heard the roar of an engine and a small dot on the road, way back towards Maskatchka, transformed itself in no time into a posh limousine. The dogs' eyes flashed with fury and the fur on their hackles glistened as they snarled at the car.

One of the dogs, probably the leader of the pack – a handsome large grey dog in his prime, with thick eyebrows and a plumey tail – was especially quick, but even he didn't manage to snap at the limousine's tyres. Still barking, the dogs followed the car as far as Eagle and Mimi's house on the corner where they came to a halt and fell quiet.

Then they all ran off in different directions except for the grey dog, who sat in the middle of the road as if to make sure the limousine didn't turn back. He stayed exactly where he was, stubbornly refusing to budge even when the tram conductor beeped at him angrily to get out of the way. In the end the dog gave a small, polite sneeze then with studied indifference walked over to where Jacob was standing and settled down comfortably in the shade.

When the street was quiet again, Jacob heard a voice.

'Darn those expensive cars! Not even bullets can make a dent in them, so what am I supposed to do with just my teeth?'

Jacob looked around, trying to work out where the voice had come from, but there was no one about. He froze. Could it *really* be…?

'Don't look around like that, as if I were the eighth wonder of the world! You are in Maskatchka now. Everything here is a bit different from what you are used to,' the voice went on.

Jacob didn't dare look at the enormous dog. He tried to remember if he had ever wished to meet talking animals – this could be exactly what his dad had warned him about, some half thought-out wish that had just come true.

'Uh-uh, we'll get nowhere like this,' the voice went on as, out of the corner of his eye, Jacob saw the dog cautiously drawing nearer. 'Hello! Welcome to Maskatchka!'

Still squinting sideways, Jacob began to believe that the dog really was speaking to him. He decided not to answer, just in case it was all a joke and Mimi was having a good laugh at him talking to himself, all alone in the middle of an empty street.

'I'm the Boss,' said the dog. 'That's what they call me here in Maskatchka. I don't remember my real name. I haven't lived with humans in a proper home for a long time. Now the streets of Maskatchka are my home and I'm the guardian of its gate.' Each word was spoken very clearly.

Jacob didn't know what to think. Still frozen to the spot he listened to the dog's friendly voice. Finally, almost without moving his lips (just in case anyone was watching) he mustered all his courage and whispered that he hadn't seen any gate.

Lifting his plumey tail high into the air, the dog replied, 'Then I'll show you everything'. And he led Jacob across the street.

Moving over towards the dogs dozing on the

patch of grass, the Boss introduced them. 'This is my gang – my friends.' The dogs answered by wagging their tails in deference while the Boss nipped at their ears or bit playfully at some of their necks.

Noticing Jacob looking more and more impressed, the Boss gave a short bark at some puppies who rolled straight over onto their backs, waving their legs in the air. 'This is my family – my boys,' he said, puffing out his chest with pride. 'And this is Bianca, my partner.'

Bianca was short-haired, once white all over but now with a touch of grey, her dark, deer-like eyes fringed with long lashes so white they were almost transparent. She smiled at him – *she*

smiled! Jacob decided that seeing a dog smile was even stranger than hearing a dog speak. Then Bianca spoke, too. He *saw* her and *heard* her but he couldn't understand a word. The Boss explained that Bianca had been born in Russia and only spoke Russian. In Maskatchka they had named her Bianca, meaning white, seeing as her previous owners hadn't bothered to give her a name, just calling her '*sobaka*' which meant 'dog' in Russian. Not a great name!

The Boss addressed some of the dogs as godfathers whilst others were uncles, cousins, aunts and sisters. Grandfather was the most elderly member of the pack. Toothless and blind, with thin fur and stiff legs, he was still greatly respected.

Indeed, The Boss told Jacob, all the others would go to him for advice at significant moments in their lives and he would sniff the air and point his tail in every direction of the compass before answering. Apparently it was Grandfather who had given his blessing for Jacob to enter Maskatchka and stay with a local family, although no one was sure why. They didn't dare ask or question his decision. Dogs *feel* such things.

Jacob's head was spinning with nerves but he found the courage to ask: 'Are you some sort of mafia gang, Boss?!'

The Maskatchka dogs started laughing. Some of them turned their heads and spoke, probably in Russian, to their neighbours who then also started laughing. Others got so carried away that they rolled about on their backs laughing, paws in the air.

'Well, maybe we are a "gang", as you put it, but certainly not a mafia one,' said the Boss. 'Us dogs are in charge round here – if it wasn't for us there would be no peace at all in Maskatchka, although we do get very angry if anyone sets out to damage our home…' The Boss dropped his head for a moment, and looked concerned before quickly straightening again proudly, as if not allowing himself the moment's weakness. 'We are not "the bad guys", we're only protecting our patch.

'So you didn't see the Gate of Maskatchka?' He looked at Jacob. 'It's right here!'

He walked between Mimi and Eagle's house on the corner and the furthest wall of the grey high-rise building, tracing an invisible line. 'Maskatchka starts here,' he said, nodding his head towards the mural on the grey building. 'On the other side is all the rest – the *Beyond*, where *City People* live.' He crossed back over the invisible line.

'Nobody can come to Maskatchka uninvited. And only those whose intentions are good are invited – as I said earlier, dogs have a keen nose for these things. We *take care* of all the rest of them.' The Boss paused meaningfully.

'Rich people's houses have high concrete walls around them to keep their riches safe inside. They settle down comfortably and spend their days surrounded by their expensive possessions. Neighbours don't know each other, separated by their high walls and they all live in constant fear of losing their belongings, always suspicious of each other.

The streets of Maskatchka are not only home to all us dogs but to all the people of Maskatchka too. We have no possessions so we can't lose anything. So the streets of Maskatchka are safe – everyone is best friends rather than feeling threatened by each other. The only people we have to worry about are the *City People,* so we watch them carefully, and if necessary scare them off by pretending to be a bit more fierce than we really are! We try to spot anyone who's up to no good. The police don't like us much though, and some of them are scared of us, so they sometimes spread rumours about us which are way over the top. Strange really when the police have far more to do *Beyond* than here in Maskatchka. Nothing bad happens here.'

'That limo – is that from *Beyond*, too?'

'Oh, yes, that darn limousine…' Boss sighed.

The dogs muttered among themselves, looking down at the ground. Only Bianca continued looking at Jacob with her big brown eyes, her snow-white eyelashes flicking silently. He could see she didn't understand a single word.

'Oh my goodness, are you actually talking *to yourself*?!' Next second, Jacob heard a scornful laugh behind him. 'Or maybe you have an imaginary friend? Hahaha!'

Startled, Jacob replied, 'Mimi! I'm not talking to myself.'

Mimi looked down at him, her arms crossed over her chest.

'I'm talking to this dog, the Boss of Maskatchka – he is *speaking* to me!'

Mimi looked at the dogs. They all remained silent.

Moving closer to examine the pack carefully,

she eventually spat out, 'Whoa, looks like you've made some great friends there!'

'No, no, he really speaks! Boss, say something to her, she *doesn't believe* me!' Jacob begged.

Flick – flick. In the silence, the only sound was that of Bianca's eyelashes. The dogs lazed about on the grass. Desperate to be believed, Jacob begged the dogs to speak, but with a snort Mimi turned on her heels and headed home.

The light had faded into dusk and it had started to rain quite heavily. The boy stayed where he was for some time, standing in the rain looking at the dogs. Bianca plainly didn't like getting wet and had gone to shelter under a tree. The others were getting soaked.

But the dogs of Maskatchka did speak – they really did! Could they possibly belong to a special protected breed of talking dogs, registered under some secret section of the Protected Species List, which only the President and certain dignitaries knew about? Gazing up into the cloudy sky, Jacob wished he could introduce the dogs to Mimi and then maybe she would want to be friends with him. Warm summer rain clouded his vision. A bolt of lightning lit up the sky.

Jacob, the bird of misfortune

The kitchen was warm and smelt deliciously of soup. Eagle told Jacob to get out of his soaking-wet clothes and hang them on the line over the stove. Mimi continued reading her book, refusing to pay any attention to her drenched cousin. Half dressed, Jacob reached up helplessly, trying in vain to hang his dripping socks high above the stove. He wondered how Mimi could keep her nose in her book with so much going on. He looked over at Eagle.

At home, Jacob loved watching his dad cook. It didn't happen often but when it did it meant his dad was off work and they would spend the day together.

Who knows what his dad was doing now. Perhaps he had forgiven Jacob for drowning Riga at the bottom of the Daugava River and had started, just a little bit, to love him again.

Eagle suggested that Jacob wash some apples for pudding.

'Have you started school yet?' Eagle asked him.

Jacob had never even gone to nursery let alone school. He and his dad had decided together that rather than going to school it was better for him to stay at home with trustworthy, if rather boring, tutors.

Mimi pricked up her ears.

'Why can't *I* study at home!?' she asked. 'It would be amazing to do nothing but read books all day … I can read all I will ever need on my own – you don't need teachers for that!'

Eagle tried to explain how sometimes teachers helped us learn things we didn't know ourselves we had to learn. That kind of learning wasn't something that came from a book. Besides, learning together with classmates was surely more fun?

'But, first, the only thing we do at school is read from books and I could do that just as well at home,' said Mimi. 'Second, being with other kids in the classroom is not that great – we all have to keep quiet the whole time and can't even share our "*experiences-ing*".' She numbered each point a finger at a time. 'Third, at the moment we're not even allowed out into the playground at break time as there might be "unsavoury types" roaming about who might offer us "dangerous substances". The entrance door is kept locked and guarded for "security reasons". I mean, really, we live in Maskatchka for goodness' sake – the safest district in Riga! How *ridikly-less* is that, Eagle?!'

No proof was needed, she finished up – she knew it all for a fact.

'Firstly, you "share experiences" not "*experiences-ing*",' said Eagle, copying her by raising a finger for each point. Secondly, it's "ridiculous", not "*ridikly-less*"… You see – you don't actually know it all!'

Mimi pouted.

'You need a *thirdly*,' she snapped. 'Otherwise the first two points don't count.'

'Is there *anything* you like about school?' Jacob asked, curious.

Mimi pretended not to hear. But then, having thought about it for a moment, she blurted out, 'Nature studies. And language isn't too bad either – but I don't know why we have to do it at school, we can all speak it anyway! Form time is more or less OK, too...'

'But best of all?' Jacob insisted.

'Break time!'

Jacob sighed. He never had those with his home tutor.

'Jacob Bird, what ARE you doing?!' Eagle stared, dumbfounded, as Jacob worked away at the apples.

Jacob was bewildered. Using a well-lathered brush in a sink full of soapy bubbles he was carefully scrubbing the fruit which was now polished to perfection!

Mimi's expression showed plainly that she thought Jacob was a complete idiot. Eagle on the other hand started roaring with such infectious laughter that soon Jacob, still baffled, joined in. And so Jacob learnt what "washing apples" meant. Apples washed with soap might be good to look at but certainly not to eat! But how was he to have known that, his home tutor had never told him. Mimi hissed that he probably couldn't even tie his own shoelaces. Eagle told her to be quiet, saying it was his fault – he should have thought that washing usually involved soap. Speaking of which, when was the last time Mimi had had a bath?

Eagle, Mimi and their new guest devoured their soup hungrily (they decided to leave apples for pudding for another time). When no more logs were fed into the stove it gradually went to sleep for the night. Eagle became lost in thought, Mimi was engrossed in a book and Jacob settled down to draw a map of his new home.

It was not a big map. Jacob would sleep on the fold-out armchair bed in the back room, which was Mimi's room. He was to 'touch nothing, pick up nothing,' she instructed him. Eagle slept on the sofa in the hallway. As you came in the front door, the kitchen was off to one side, the warmth from the stove filling the whole flat (although it didn't quite reach as far as the chilly blackness of the bathroom walls across the hallway). The windows were thick with grime, a haze of murky light weaving its way through the rooms. Jacob recorded all this on his *Map of Mimi and Eagle's Flat*.

When it was time for bed, Jacob lifted his clothes off the line only to discover he couldn't find his left sock. 'Bad sock!' Jacob muttered as he put the right one on and continued hunting for the left.

Eagle joined in the search, agreeing that it really was a bad sock if the right one was good, and yes it was silly that the heart should be on the wrong side. Mimi thought that only little children talked such nonsense.

Jacob was too tired to point out the reasons why he was already quite grown up. Eventually Mimi also joined the hunt for the missing sock and happened to look in the soup pot.

'I DON'T BELIEVE IT!' she shrieked in horror. 'Who else would hang his clothes over the cooking pot – only one of you two; you're both about as bright as a newborn baby!'

She fished Jacob's left sock out of the soup they had just eaten and waved it in front his nose.

'Jacob Bird,' she started saying in grave tones, but the she gave up. 'But hey, you aren't an ordinary bird! You are a *bird of misfortune*! Jacob Lame Duck – that's what I'll call you!'

She was so horrible! His dad didn't love him, Miss Freckle didn't want to be friends with him, he could do nothing right and didn't understand a thing! Jacob was desperately unhappy. But he didn't have time to feel unhappy for long...

'I might be horrid but at least no one has to babysit me – I know it all and I can do anything!

'And don't call me Miss Freckle – I hate my freckly nose!'

Mimi stamped her foot and marched to her room, making a show of locking the door behind her.

Jacob realised he had probably said it all out

loud again. Back home in the apartment on Brīvības Street, he often talked to imaginary playmates, acting out all the parts if necessary. Sometimes he got carried away and would talk out loud to himself even when his dad was there. But then his dad would have debates with himself too when he was deep in thought, muttering away under his breath. Other times he'd seen his dad pull faces at himself in the mirror – showing off his perfectly straight teeth – then unsuccessfully try to reproduce the same smile at parties for the benefit of ladies who also had flashing white teeth. When Jacob found him out, his dad defended himself by saying that, after all, he was talking to the most intelligent person in the world. It was true – his dad really was the most intelligent person in the world.

Eagle thought that there would be no harm in his nephew sharing the narrow sofa bed with him for one night. Jacob tried really hard to feel *deeply unhappy* but found he couldn't keep it up for long. It had been a long day, filled with adventure, and in no time at all he was sound asleep.

Searching for the former shadow

Morning arrived with a deafening noise. A straight beam of sunlight stretched across the pillows, vapourising sleep from Jacob's eyes. He opened them to see the room transformed into something rather like an enormous lilac bush with millions of white dust particles whirling around. But the sun had completed its mission and disappeared behind the clouds.

Eagle must have only just got up – the dent in the sofa where he had been sleeping was still warm and smelled of tobacco and fresh sawdust.

Going into the kitchen, Jacob was greeted by a

strange scene. Eagle, dressed only in his underpants, a new pair of socks and a once-black suit jacket, was standing patiently in the middle of the kitchen while Miss Freck ... sorry, Mimi, stood on a kitchen stool carefully moving the head of an extraordinarily loud vacuum cleaner over his jacket.

'GOOD MORNING, MR DUCK,' his uncle shouted over the noise of the vacuum cleaner. 'WELCOME TO MIMI AND EAGLE'S DRYCLEANING SERVICE – ONE, TWO, THREE AND YOU ARE CLEAN!'

It was the UNIQUE MASKATCHKA DRY CLEANER'S and there was no other like it anywhere in the world – Eagle could vouch for that, seeing as he was a sailor.

Mimi was in unusually high spirits, every so often doing a little dance on the narrow stool.

'EAGLE'S BEING SENT TO TRY OUT FOR A NEW JOB! HE'S GOING TO BE A SECURITY GUARD' she sang. 'FOR A SHOP OR A CAR PARK OR MAYBE A FORESTRY GUARD FOR TALL TREES!'

Those pirates must have really frightened him, Jacob mused, as he looked at the long scar wreathing down Eagle's bare leg. Why else would he abandon such an amazing job, sailing gigantic ships laden with secret cargo of great importance?

Suddenly, a loose button on Eagle's best jacket came off and was sucked noisily up the vacuum cleaner's long nozzle. Oh no, the party was over!

'Eagle won't get the job without a button,' said Mimi. She was beside herself. She started rummaging energetically in the belly of the vacuum cleaner looking for the missing button, causing a massive cloud of dust to bellow out of it. It settled in every crease of her father's best jacket and left Eagle himself covered from head to toe in powdery grime, just the whites of his eyes shining through the muck. A great amount of activity followed, with dusters and the vacuum cleaner again – Eagle stood no chance of being offered the job looking like that!

All the while, Jacob fidgeted about impatiently, kicking his heels by the front door. Then, unnoticed due to the mighty dust cloud, he slipped out onto the streets of Maskatchka.

Jacob was all alone in the world!

It was one of those windy days you could never be sure about. Clouds were pushing each other about restlessly in the sky, giving each other bright purple bruises. The dogs must be off on a tour around their patch, leaving the Maskatchka Gate unguarded and unmarked in any way. Jacob breathed in and positioned himself at the Gate with one foot in Maskatchka and the other *Beyond*; mainly to find out if it would feel weird to be on both sides at the same time.

The sun peeped out for a while from behind the clouds. But threatening black shadows spread like ink along the bottom of the houses and dark, flickering shadow babies nibbled the patch of juicy grass under the distant trees. When the curtain of clouds descended again, the shadows put their tails between their legs and disappeared without a trace. Jacob bent down and looked between his legs to see what his shadow was doing.

Still with his head between his legs, Jacob heard Mimi's jeering voice again, 'Morning work-out session?!

'Incredible! The pasty city boy is into keep fit!' she called out to Eagle who, not looking entirely presentable, just waved at the two children before hurrying off, hopefully to his new place of work.

Jacob couldn't help himself and so he confided in his cousin.

'Mimi … I haven't got a shadow anymore!' he whispered.

Mimi, her freckled nose stuck high in the air, stared at the boy in silence. Yet again, here was something this poor little weakling, this Jacob Lame Duck didn't understand, didn't know or couldn't do! She rolled her eyes and circled Jacob nonchalantly. The second time she started looking more carefully. After circling him a third time, she was doing her best to hide her bewilderment. With all the care of a detective, Mimi checked Jacob's heels and feet to make sure the shadow wasn't hiding underneath. She calculated how tall he was and tried to figure out how long his shadow should be. The calculations lasted several minutes with Mimi raising, bending and counting on her fingers. When she had finished she announced:

'Your shadow has definitely disappeared. A Lame Duck like you might even lose his head if it wasn't screwed on.'

Jacob wasn't sure why but he had started crying. In truth, he had never even liked his shadow. It was dark and scary, rude and bad-mannered and … and only ever thought of itself; what was the name for it? *Shell-fish* – Mimi prompted – that's what it was.

'There's no such thing as a shadow-less person!

Everything, living or not, has a shadow. If you don't have a shadow, you don't exist!' Mimi stated. 'Are you sure you are *real*?'

Jacob thought about it for a moment. As far as he was aware, he had always been real.

Mimi sighed: 'Well, what are we to do now, Jacob Lame Duck? If you are really real and you've lost your shadow, we had better go and find it!'

She seemed excited by the prospect of an adventure and persuaded Jacob they needed to go on an expedition. The Expedition needed a name, and a good one at that.

Mimi came up with "Expedition in Search of the Useless Boy's Former Shadow". Jacob wasn't too keen on that, thinking that "Expedition in Search of the Wonder Boy's Former Shadow" sounded better, but Mimi was not to be swayed. They eventually agreed to call it the "Expedition in Search of the Boy's Former Shadow".

Their first stop was not too far away.

'Lost, abandoned shadows probably hang about in huffy huddles on stairwells – not a bunch of fun creatures you'd want to run into,' said Mimi as they slipped into the hall of their home. 'Which is why it's always so unwelcoming here!'

The stairwell was unlit. Dampness oozed from hidden corners like acid sweat. Jacob felt dizzy, a foul taste in his mouth. It had never crossed his mind that the reason his heart beat so horribly fast in dark stairwells was because lost, angry shadows lurked there. No sooner had palpitations sprung to his mind than his heart started beating on the wrong side of his chest. Jacob whispered that he didn't b-believe h-his sh-shadow w-would be s-somewhere so un-unwelcoming. Maybe it had slipped unnoticed onto the streets of Maskatchka and was now wandering along somewhere or romping about with the dogs. Could his shadow really be out there on its own?

Mimi told him calmly that he was quite right. Before Jacob had time to answer, amazed that *Mimi had agreed with him*, she went on to say that his shadow was definitely too wimpy to tough it out with such battle-hardened companions and suggested looking somewhere more suited to a scaredy-cat.

The next stop on their expedition was the demolition site at Number 13. A house had once stood there but no one wanted to live in it, thinking Number 13 was unlucky. One morning, the building just wasn't there anymore. It was rumoured that it had just vanished into the air, others claimed that it had been hit by an evil, one-eyed comet. Every so often, someone unfamiliar with the area fell into the hole as if it were a trap.

Jacob's shadow hadn't fallen in so they went on their way.

It turned out that Maskatchka was more pleasant than Jacob had first thought. The Daugava River ran down one side. He found himself waiting on its green banks for the tall ships with their bulging bellies to appear at any moment, pebbles plunging into the water with a deep splosh. The heart of Maskatchka was alive with living, breathing parks and overgrown apple orchards. The paving slabs on the silent streets, which glittered on rainy nights like snakeskin in the glow of street lamps, were now sun-baked and clacked like piano keys. Lazy cats lounged in the open windows of low wooden houses – the windows reflecting the cloudy heavens rather than the more usual walls opposite and pulse of neon lights. You could hear the sound of your thoughts as you walked, or at least you could if Mimi wasn't there – her constant fizz of chatter was like a babbling brook.

'What on earth have you been up to to make your dad stop loving you?' she asked, aiming her toe at another stone.

'Everything I wish for comes true,' Jacob replied.

Mimi stared at him in disbelief, forgetting all about the stone.

'Everything?!'

Jacob *absolutely* had to find a way of proving it to her.

'All it would take is for me to say that Riga is

ready and the whole city would sink to the bottom of the Daugava River. I can make disasters happen by wishing for them. But I *don't want* them to happen.'

Mimi snorted.

'I don't believe you! And anyhow, what's the point in wishing for something like that? If your wishes come true, you should wish for something that would help other people!'

'Oh, I get it!' Jacob exclaimed. He understood. There had to be a more *sensible* wish.

Then he had a wonderful idea. How about wishing for all the sweets, cakes and chocolate bars in the whole world to appear before them, right there and then? His mouth started watering at the thought.

'No! If whatever you wish comes true, you need to get your brain in gear and I don't think yours is working very well at the moment. Can you imagine what would happen? Where would they all go? We would both be *crushed* – have you any idea how many sweets there are on the planet?!? Enough to cover an entire continent! Not to mention the fact that if your wish did come true, Mascatchka would be covered in chocolate and it would take me years to get it all out of my hair and...'

With the tide of Mimi's chatter washing over him, Jacob reasoned that if he was to try and help other people, he should wish for everyone to be happy. So he should wish for *all the wishes in the world to come true.*

Wasn't that a good idea?

'Don't be silly! What if someone wished horrible things on other people? Just think of the consequences! And it would be all your fault!'

Mimi was insufferable!! Surely there was something he could wish for that didn't have a dark side? Was there nothing without a shadowy side?

Jacob was the only person on the planet at that moment who didn't have a shadowy side, Mimi pointed out. Jacob was dumbstruck – he *had wished* for his shadow to disappear! Now, all he had to do was wish for his shadow to re-appear!

'Where did you last see your shadow?' asked Mimi, shaking her head in disbelief.

Jacob seemed to remember seeing it the night before at the Maskatchka Gate.

'Oh, of course! The shadow was not invited into Maskatchka so had to stay outside!'

As soon as they reached the Gate, Jacob – a little out of breath – started shouting, 'Former Shadow of the Wonder Boy, you are very welcome to Maska...' only to be interrupted by Mimi, telling him to forget it. There was no way they were calling it the shadow of the *wonder boy* – they had agreed. Jacob tried to defend himself – it was only a polite way of saying hello!

While they argued, the wind blew the billowing clouds off to one side and the sun appeared high above their heads. In the blink of an eye, the contours of Maskatchka started to glow brightly, reflections of glittering gold domes from the cloisters across the road flashing in its windows. The shape of Jacob's shadow appeared at his back.

'Hurray!' Jacob exclaimed, delighted.

Mimi watched the shadow, lost in thought, then squinted up at the sun.

The brighter the sunshine, the darker the shadow – its glistening black sheen was almost blinding. The Former Shadow looked amazing!

See, Jacob said to Mimi, all his wishes really did come true! Mimi responded with no more than a wise, 'Hmm.'

'So if I wanted, I could wish for my dad to start loving me again!'

Mimi remained suspiciously quiet about the whole thing.

It was lovely in Maskatchka. Safe too – he could wander where he wanted through the streets – but only until his dad reappeared and loved him again, which he would very soon.

Waiting for his dad to come back for him, Jacob drew a map on the pavement of all he had seen in Maskatchka.

TO BEYOND
GATES OF MASKATCHKA
LONELY TRAM STOP
MURALS
DOGS
BRIDGE

CHURCH
PARK
MOLITION
CAVE
13.
ACADEMY
OF DREAMERS
SOME HARMLESS
CITY
PEOPLE
CLOISTER
DAUGAVA RIVER

The duck who didn't have time to feel unhappy

There was still no sign of Jacob's dad. If he had time, Jacob would sit on the edge of the pavement feeling sorry for himself about how very unhappy he was. As it turned out, he didn't have much time for that because of what happened next.

The shiny limousine screeched to a halt at the Gates of Maskatchka leaving black tyre marks all over the white chalk map of the district that Jacob had drawn. The chauffeur got out of the limo and marched over to him. The whole world seemed to be reflected in the chauffeur's patent leather shoes. His long nose expanded like an enormous cloud above them: the nostrils the size of black holes in outer space. He was wearing a dark uniform with white shoulder braid, white gloves and a matching hat with a shiny black peak. Without saying a word, the tall, thin chauffeur reached out long fingers and took the chalk from Jacob's hand. He snapped it in two before writing, in big letters, next to the map of Maskatchka:

**GRAND MASTER SKYLER
SCRAPER RULES HERE**

The uniformed chauffeur then handed the chalk carefully back to Jacob and the limousine quietly entered Maskatchka unhindered.

Mimi had watched the scene like a small, frightened animal but now she snatched the chalk from Jacob and ran to the wall where she scrubbed out some of the chauffeur's words and, correcting herself several times, wrote something else in its place. When at last she was satisfied that she had got it right, she let the chalk fall to the ground and vanished into Maskatchka without uttering a word.

GRAND MOTHER SKY~~SCRAPER~~ SCRAPER RULES HERE

Annoyed that he'd been left on his own while real life was going on elsewhere (he used to imagine real life unfolding outside the dining-room window – now it was wherever Mimi happened to be), Jacob walked through the streets of Maskatchka in the hope of finding it.

Instead, he came across the Boss and his pack who were pacing restlessly outside the Academy of Dreamers – this was what they called the place where *City People* came to learn about the Arts, Theatre and Film. Only *they* yearned to learn everything there was to learn. And it was only after long years in the pursuit of wisdom that they realised no one could know everything and then they grew melancholy. One of the dogs, the mongrel with no schooling and no teeth called Granddad, was the only one of the gang to understand this. Seeing as they were all so melancholy, the dreamers were perfectly harmless and posed no threat to Maskatchka, the Boss confirmed. Indeed, they were the only *City People* to be charmed by the district. This was the place where melancholy love songs were written, forlorn poets wandered and ancient tragedies were performed in the apple orchards. So it couldn't really be said that the dogs of Maskatchka – who watched all this from beneath the bushes or from the tops of derelict houses – were an entirely uneducated bunch.

The Boss went on to explain that they weren't there to watch the harmless dreamers – the fact was that while on a tour of duty round their patch to check up on the other *City People*, Bianca had somehow gone missing.

'Again,' the Boss sighed, sounding resigned. 'Sometimes Bianca catches sight of some welcoming-looking family and goes off wagging her tail. Even though it has brought her nothing but bad luck and unhappiness, she misses human company so much that she sometimes gets separated from the pack. Other times she gets lost in thought, looking through the window of someone's home, longing to return to a family to look after her. Once in the park she got distracted by a hat a lady had lost – she spent hours modelling it, feeling even more beautiful than usual – while all the time we were searching high and low for her. She has a very poor sense of smell, poor thing, no doubt because of her mistreatment at the hands of humans. So when she gets separated from the pack, unable even to speak our language, she can't find her way back… But then she will suddenly just reappear. There's nothing we can do, we just have to wait patiently.'

'Mum's been disappearing more often lately,' whined one of the twin puppies. The Boss silenced him with a growl. Jacob couldn't tell which of the twins it was – Zephyr or Sapphire.

Spotting his chance, Jacob asked the Boss why he hadn't spoken in front of Mimi the night before. The Boss growled.

'That girl is a naughty young whippersnapper!' he said. 'She thinks we are a bunch of "good for nothing, scruffy rascals" and no good at all as guard dogs. She fancies herself as the best guard of Maskatchka, that's the trouble! Ha! She won't work alongside us because she thinks she knows it all. Can you imagine? What sort of guard could she possibly make? Bah! No sharp teeth, no speed, no quick reactions!' The Boss gave a quick demonstration, chasing after his own tail. 'One day, Mimi accused us of not being proper dogs because we talk, saying, "Real dogs don't talk, they act." From that day on, we've done exactly as she said and refuse to speak to her!'

Granddad suddenly started sniffing the air and swishing his tail meaningfully. The extraordinary pack of dogs growled as a figure came round the corner – someone who always managed to be in the middle of whatever was going on...

Mimi bowled confidently up to the pack.

The Boss did everything he could to avoid her. First he went and scuffled about with one of the godfathers, then one of the uncles or maybe a cousin. Then he went and marked out his territory on the corner of the Academy for Dreamers with his usual signature.

Mimi rolled her eyes.

'Can we move on to *important* matters now?!' she said, clenching her fists at her sides.

Looking disinterested, the Boss struck a pose in front of Mimi. The first dog of Maskatchka still had tufts of fur from the scrap sticking out of his mouth.

'In case you didn't realise, while you were fooling about like a pup and relieving yourself where you shouldn't,' Mimi snorted, 'a limousine drove straight through the gates of Maskatchka which you'd left unguarded, unprotected! And, if that wasn't bad enough, it would seem he has managed to put his dreadful plan into action completely undisturbed! And we all know what that means!'

The Boss spat the clump of fur out in astonishment and one of his front paws began to twitch, almost imperceptibly. The pack took up attack position and waited for his command. The atmosphere was electrifying; the dogs' fur seemed to bristle with sparks.

Jacob had no idea what it all meant!

'Skyler Scraper, the owner of the limousine, has his own plans for Maskatchka,' Mimi explained. 'He wants to build the tallest skyscrapers in the world here; destroying our parks, cutting down our apple orchards, demolishing our wooden homes and concreting over our gardens in the process. If his plans go ahead, Maskatchka will be re-named Skyscraper Forest, with as many skyscrapers as trees in a forest! Looking down from the heights of Skyscraper Forest, the rest of the world will be no more than a tiny, insignificant valley below all the high-rise buildings.

Which is why Grand Master Scraper, or should we say, Grand Conman Skyscraper, wants to get rid of everyone standing in the way of his plans for Maskatchka. First of all, he wants to throw out everyone living here. Skyscraper Forest is going to be an exclusive development separated from the rest of the world by a thick wall, so he wants all of us to pack our bags and disappear. Secondly, the streets of Maskatchka will be transformed into dangerous highways – living in the streets will be out of the question and children won't be allowed out to play unless a grown-up is with them. And how can children play with grown-ups watching!' Mimi counted the points on her fingers again.

'Thirdly, he wants to do away with the tiresome guards of Maskatchka because, of course, there is no place for stray dogs on such an exclusive development. You can imagine what that will mean for the guard dogs of Maskatchka, can't you? They will get packed off to cages in the city dog pound with all the other strays – not a happy ending for a bunch of good-for-nothing, scruffy rascals!'

Zephyr and Sapphire pushed their tails between their legs and whined pitifully.

'ENOUGH!' the Boss growled.

Mimi was startled. The dogs had not spoken to her for so long she had started to wonder if they ever really had.

She looked from the dogs to Jacob in surprise.

The Boss pointed at Mimi with the tip of his

tail and said to his pack: 'We will not live in cages in the dog shelter! We have guarded Maskatchka up til now and we will keep on guarding it!' He thumped his paw on the ground as some people hit a table with their fists.

The pack went wild with applause, barking and wagging their tails enthusiastically against the wall of the Academy of Dreamers.

'And how do you think you will carry on guarding Maskatchka with no more than your old teeth?' Mimi raged. 'At least I have EFFE-ACTUAL means to fight with.'

The Boss bit back his shame, then yawned widely, displaying rows of impressive teeth. Who was known in Maskatchka as the BOSS if not him?!? The first dog of Maskatchka snapped his jaws and chased away some pigeons quietly pecking at the ground next to him. The puppies joined in, delighted.

'Hey!' Mimi rolled her eyes furiously. 'Can you please try and grow up?'

'Growing up hurts!' the puppies complained, licking their back paws which ached with growing pains.

Then Zephyr and Sapphire started laughing so hard that Jacob almost shook with laughter too (he wasn't used to hearing dogs laugh). They explained they were imagining Mimi as a baby looking just as she did now; crossly shouting out orders which no one took any notice of as there were no grown-ups around. Furiously Mimi tried to make herself taller, determined to be heard.

'I only talked to you to share my plans for saving Maskatchka, but it seems you're not bothered about saving your skins … or fur or whatever!' Mimi scowled before spitting out, 'Conman Skyscraper can't put his plans into action without the help of us

locals who know Maskatchka like the backs of our
hands … or paws! Which means he must have
planted a SPY in our midst!' Mimi looked round in
triumph, enjoying the fact that finally she had
everyone's attention.

The puppies stopped frolicking and hiccupped.
After a moment of tense silence, the shocked pack
started whispering.

'It can't be…' the Boss growled, squinting
suspiciously at his mates. 'Who was the last one to
be invited into Maskatchka?'

Jacob looked at his shadow in disbelief. His shadow couldn't be the spy, surely?

The dogs let out a horrible growling noise. Jacob put his head in his hands and shrank to the ground. If the dogs were going to tear him limb from limb, he would be very gritty for them to chew, he thought. But before he had time to explain it was all a big mistake he heard the dogs howling to each other:

'BIANCA!'

'Bianca is in the limousine!'

'She's been KIDNAPPED!'

Skyscraper Forest

The dogs ran like the wind. The Boss ran as fast as he could to keep up with the limousine, howling in desperation without the slightest care for his position or rank. Bianca looked pitifully at her mate's futile attempts to snap at the tyres, her nose pressed up against the rear window.

The puppies followed on behind. Jacob urged them on but there was no way they could keep up with the pack of dogs. When at last Jacob caught up with the puppies, he grabbed them around their middles and picked them up.

Mimi lagged behind too as the raging dogs of Maskatchka tore ahead at incredible speed. There was a terrible commotion; the limousine was honking its horn, the dogs were barking like mad and Mimi was shouting out orders no one could hear or take any notice of. Then Mimi darted off into a side street, beckoning Jacob to follow.

'I know where the limousine is heading – let's try to get there first!'

Jacob had great difficulty keeping up with Mimi as Zephyr and Sapphire, although only puppies, were heavy and kept licking his face. As they ran through the tiny streets, Jacob tried to remember the way.

Suddenly they came to a huge out-of-the-way park where there was a great deal of feverish activity. Jacob stood frozen to the spot. Then he breathed in sharply. Immense, ancient trees were being felled here, one after another; frightened birds fluttered out of the foliage and tiny chicks, too small to fly, tumbled helplessly from their nests. The trunks of mighty trees that crashed to the ground with an enormous thud were being sawn up and carted away. Colossal, ugly holes were being dug where the trees had once stood. A crooked sign at the entrance to the site read:

WELCOME TO SKYSCRAPER WOOD
YOU'RE BANNED FROM THE
NEIGHBOURHOOD!

And below this:

WHAT ARE YOU STARING AT?
THE TALLEST BUILDINGS OF THE FUTURE
WILL BE BUILT RIGHT HERE
WHERE YOU ARE STANDING.
SO DISAPPEAR!

Trying to hide his amazement, Jacob quickly closed his mouth. Next to the sign was a drawing showing what the park would look like in the future. In the place of trees rose infinitely tall buildings, their spikes puncturing the black clouds above. All the lawns were smothered with gleaming black tarmac. The tightly packed buildings crowded out the nearby church so much that the cross on top of its steeple was hidden from view.

The beautiful park was to be turned into a concrete jungle like those Jacob had seen in science-fiction movies. Up until then, Jacob had seen very few parks as beautiful as this one and the thought of losing it was terrible. He could see that until now you could have played all sorts of wonderful games here without doing anything you weren't allowed to!

As they glanced around, Jacob and Mimi noticed that other signs had been put up in nearby backyards and gardens. Right now they were full of lush greenery, but it seemed like they were somehow waiting for their doom, among the spread of tarmac and cement. Yet more signs showed shopping centres taking the place of the lovely old houses, shopping centres identical to the many others dotted round Riga that Jacob had visited with his dad. Other illustrations showed Maskatchka quite changed from how it was now – no longer brimming with joy and life but instead as dead as the forest, which had been felled right down to the very last tree. The shiny skyscrapers on the signs only made the spooky feeling worse. There was not a single tree, lawn, park or garden in any of the illustrations, no children playing on the streets, and definitely no packs of talking dogs – there was not so much as a cat lazing behind a skyscraper window. The whole scene looked unwelcoming to any form of human or animal habitation, the only sign of life being the all-seeing eyes of the security cameras.

The puppies clearly thought that only humans could come up with something so hideous, and gave a heart-rending yelp as they watched their favourite tree fall to the ground. Day in, day out they had helped their father mark out the Maskatchka territory, sharing their own doggy bulletin board where all the local dogs could leave messages and swap news.

Thinking it would be a good idea to look for a hiding place in case the limousine appeared, Mimi led Jacob behind a green rubbish bin. It wasn't a great hiding place as it was no longer surrounded by greenery, but there was nothing else. Mimi had been right as before long the shiny black limousine glided into the park. The car had obviously been faster than the dogs. There was no sign of them.

The now-familiar chauffeur unfolded himself like a spider from the limousine, followed from the passenger seat by a tall, broad-shouldered man wearing a suit and dark sunglasses. Must be a bodyguard, Jacob thought. He had seen important-looking guys with sunglasses like that in films. The chauffeur opened the back door of the limo and Jacob waited, holding his breath, for his first glimpse of the evil Grand Conman Skyscraper, but no! the bodyguard stepped in front, shielding the scoundrel from sight. Mimi whispered that she had never seen Master Conman with a bodyguard before (maybe her EFFE-ACTUAL means of intimidation had got him scared, she said). She also noted that Grand Conman Skyscraper had not grown very tall. She was right. A short, plump figure could just be seen hurrying along behind the bodyguard's legs – but seeing as the guard was very good at his job, Jacob didn't manage to see much more. Then, her head hanging low, Bianca jumped out of the car. Grand Conman Skyscraper held the snow-white dog on a jangling chain of shiny metal.

The puppies tried to smother their whines.

'He has our mum on a *lead*!' Sapphire exploded – there was no greater humiliation for a street dog!

Bianca trotted obediently at the heels of the three men, following them into a nearby school.

'They must have done a secret deal with the teachers,' Mimi whispered. 'He must be trying to hammer out his plans for the most EFFE-ACTUAL ways of destroying our homes while he's in there! I'm not sure about that as yet, but I do know that he turns up here almost every day!

'OK, we can come out of hiding now,' she added, glancing at her watch. 'We have a couple of hours. He usually stays in there until about five o'clock.'

'What now?' Jacob asked.

Hackles raised and looking as menacing as possible, Sapphire growled, 'Let's get them!'

'Fighting won't work, we have to outwit them!' Mimi said, trying to calm him down. It sounded like she had it all planned out.

The puppies suddenly pricked up their ears and started wagging their tails as they picked up a familiar scent. Noses to the ground, sniffing for footprints, the pack of talking dogs could be seen in the distance moving in the direction of the park. The Boss was limping.

The puppies, sure that their father would sort the baddies out, raced over and told him what they had just seen.

'You bet I will!' the Boss promised, although his voice betrayed a note of uncertainty.

The large dog hobbled towards Mimi.

'Just a bump,' he reassured Jacob, as the boy looked with concern at the dog's injured leg.

The Boss ran his eyes over the pack before turning to Mimi.

'We must join forces,' he said quietly. 'Put our disagreements behind us. We must have a united front if we are to defend our home. We'll only get a chance to save Bianca from the paws … no, the hands of Master Conman Skyscraper if we work together. Our "old teeth" are not as good as your EFFECTIVE means, Mimi.'

Mimi said nothing. The Boss raised his voice.

'We'll send him packing from Maskatchka, we'll make him disappear with his tyres squeaking! We're going to make it IMPOSSIBLE for Grand Conman Skyscraper to stay here!'

The dogs cheered.

'What do you say to that, Mimi?'

Mimi was looking suspiciously at the dogs, as if she was thinking it through.

'Point number one,' she began, holding up her little finger. 'There will be no pointless tyre biting! Just look at you, you've done more damage to yourselves than to that car. Point number two, would you mind not leaving your signature on every street corner? You just give yourselves away! Point number three, it's all very well you being talking dogs but please don't TALK BACK so much and do as I tell you.'

The Boss gnashed his teeth. He looked at his puppies. Through gritted teeth, he said what no one ever expected to hear.

'Okay then, we'll do it your way.'

They shook on it, Mimi taking the Boss's paw in her hand.

'Can you imagine anything worse – Skyscraper Forest!' The Boss sneezed and looked around at the scene of desolation that had once been the park. 'We will not allow our home to be transformed into a place of worship to immeasurable quantities of cement, with not a living soul left in the park!'

The dogs went wild despite not really understanding the Boss's use of metaphors, which he had overheard at a poetry soirée at the Academy of Dreamers.

Mimi silenced the dogs with a wave of her hand. The Boss looked away but continued watching out of the corner of his eye.

'Let "Operation Free Maskatchka" commence!' said Mimi.

The dogs looked at each other in approval – what a great name for their mission!

The first task for Operation Free Maskatchka, namely *The Very Serious and Especially Important First Steps*, Mimi entrusted to Zephyr and Sapphire. The puppies were so excited that they could neither sit nor stand still, but kept rubbing and wriggling against each other, completely unable to concentrate on what they were being told. But Mimi whispered something in their ears and ordered them come back as quickly as possible. The puppies rolled down the hill to the busy construction site and, unnoticed, lost themselves amongst the workmen.

The Boss grew restless, glancing mistrustfully at Mimi. After seemingly endless minutes of tension, the Boss let out a sigh of relief as both puppies came tumbling back, safe and sound. Zephyr had a can of white paint between his teeth, Sapphire a blue one. Sapphire tried to beat his brother back to the pack but only succeeded in tripping over, splashing a huge splat of blue paint over his nose. At least it would be easier to tell them apart now, Jacob thought.

'Good job, boys!' Mimi exclaimed and scratched behind their ears.

The Boss swelled with pride, cuffing his boys' sides to show how pleased he was: Sapphire rolled straight over onto his back while Zephyr was so excited he accidently splashed wee on the ground before hiding between one of his aunt's legs in embarrassment.

'And now – let's get going!'

The children took down all Master Conman Skyscraper's notices and the dogs, dipping their tails into the can of white paint, painted over the writing. Then they moved on to the blue paint, dipping their tails in once more and using them to write in graffiti-style lettering the message that Mimi dictated:

MASKATCHKA WILL NOT BE LOST IN A
FOREST OF SKYSCRAPERS!
GET LOST, GRAND MASTER
SKYLER SCRAPER!

For a free Maskatchka

One of the uncles, unable to stop himself any longer, started to snap at the posh limousine. Circling the gleaming car, he just couldn't help himself and started biting at a tyre – he was soon joined by another dog, then a third and a fourth, each of them attacking their own tyre. At first they screwed up their noses and spat out the horrible-tasting rubber, only to decide shortly after that it tasted like liquorice allsorts. (Eagle had once given the dogs the liquorice sweets he brought back from a sea voyage to Scandinavia, and which Mimi had declared were "unsuitable for human consumption".)

By the time Mimi saw what they were up to, it was already too late. The tyres had been reduced to no more than four heaps of well-chewed shreds of rubber.

'There is *no way* we can leave the limousine looking like that!' she said. The dogs hung their heads in shame.

'Seeing as you've made a start dismantling it, we have no choice but to finish the job. We'll move what is left to its rightful place!'

The dogs looked at each other and yelped in excitement.

Mimi summoned another meeting and selected the fastest dogs from the Boss's gang – three bony Russian windhounds.

'Godfather Boreas, you will go to the north of Maskatchka, Uncle Notus will go to the south, and Uncle Eurus will run to the east.'

'And who will go to the west?' Jacob asked.

'Zephyr will go to the near side of Maskatchka, here to the west,' Mimi resolved, turning to the puppy, while the blue stain on the tip of Sapphire's nose turned almost green with envy. 'Zephyr, round up the neighbourhood boys and bring them back here, quickly! You windhounds are to search out the boys in your areas who'll be the best at playing thieves!'

Quietly the Boss explained to Jacob that occasionally they got the most gifted residents of Maskatchka to play the parts of thieves and robbers and scare away any undesirables. Jacob thought it an excellent tactic.

Little Zephyr turned out to be faster than the three windhounds put together. He came back with three fiery-haired, freckle-faced boys – the Toughnut brothers – the greatest troublemakers in the area, maybe in the whole of Riga! This wouldn't be the first time that people from *Beyond* were on the receiving end of one of their pranks, the Boss remarked. One hot summer day the Toughnut boys had poured tar on the pavement by the tram stop and the *City People* had all stuck fast waiting for their tram. A pair of quality ladies shoes and two little pairs of lapdog's bootees were still wedged in the tarmac there.

Mimi whispered something to the brothers and they all laughed in delight. All three had wide gaps between their big milk teeth and every so often they would spit through them in an elegant arc.

When the windhounds came back with three more 'thieves' in tow, Mimi clambered up onto the roof of the limousine and silenced all those present with a wave of her hand.

'We don't have much time! In half an hour, Grand Master Conman Skyscraper will leave the school with his accomplices and Bianca, who he has kidnapped! Your task is to take the limousine to pieces in just thirty minutes!' she ordered. The Toughnut boys were itching to get started and the would-be thieves rubbed their hands together in anticipation.

They were finished in less than half the time. After just ten minutes, the limousine was a heap of metal, the sort you might see in a wrecker's yard. They really were the best pretend thieves ever, even better than the real actors Jacob had seen in films – they were so good he completely forgot that they were only play-acting! Where the shiny limousine had once stood was now a pile of spare parts, making you want to construct a dream car of your own. The 'thieves' would have loved to take pieces of the beautiful vehicle back to their garages as trophies, or sell them quickly at the Latgalīte flea market, but the pile looked so impressive it would definitely send the right message to Maskatchka's enemy. Mimi then positioned a notice where the limousine had been parked.

CARRIED OUT AS PART OF "OPERATION FREE MASKATCHKA"!
FEEL FREE TO USE A WHEELBARROW IN FUTCHA!
IT WILL GIVE YOU SOMETHING TO DO WHILE WE BEATCHYA!

Mimi, Jacob, the Boss and his gang hid behind the green rubbish bins again and waited. At five o'clock, just as Mimi had said, the trio came out of the building accompanied by Bianca on her lead.

Arriving at the point where Master Conman's expensive, shiny limousine had been parked, the three men stopped in their tracks.

The children watched as Grand Conman Skyscraper ordered his bodyguard to read the notice propped up by the wreckage. He probably had poor eyesight because of his old age and couldn't see to read the writing himself. The bodyguard then started reading all the other notices penned by Mimi, Jacob and the Maskatchka dogs.

Grand Conman Skyscraper was beside himself with rage. They couldn't make out exactly what he was screaming but they had a good view of the short, chubby man as he leapt about waving his hands and feet in fury, his face as red as a beetroot.

He must have given his chauffeur the sack – seeing as there was no limousine for him to drive anymore – because the tall, skinny man walked off, head hung low.

Conman Skyscraper shook his fist in the air

and, gripping Bianca by her lead he headed over to the site foreman's prefab hut with the bodyguard at his side. It looked like he turned the foreman out of his own hut on the spot, going in and slamming the door behind him.

The children and dogs crept out of their hiding place.

'How exactly do we beat them?' the Boss asked.

Mimi scratched her head, playing for time.

'Well…'

'DON'T TELL ME THAT YOU DON'T HAVE A PLAN!' the Boss barked. He hated feeling so helpless!

'The important thing is to look like we have a plan – so the enemy gets scared and tries to second-guess us. But whatever he comes up with he's doomed to fail as we haven't actually got a plan for him to guess!'

The dogs were nodding their heads in approval – it was very clever.

'I *knew* it would be a mistake to join forces with Mimi!' the Boss huffed. 'We have to *do* something! We can't just sit on our paws and hope that Conman Skyscraper's efforts to foil some *non-existent plan* don't work!'

'Plans!' Jacob exclaimed suddenly.

Mimi and the dogs looked at the little boy in confusion. Jacob tried with all his might to focus his concentration on the idea starting to hatch in his mind.

'To build Skyscraper Forest, they'll need plans and maps for the layout, won't they?'

'Yes, so what?'

If Master Conman Skyscraper believed they had some terrible, grisly, horrible plan to free Maskatchka, he would no doubt go to great lengths to discover exactly what it was. In that case, he would be too busy to supervise the construction of Skyscraper Forest properly. And if that was true, all they needed to do was switch his plans for Skyscraper Forest with those for Free Maskatchka and all the builders working for the enemy would build for the good of Maskatchka without suspecting a single thing.

'Mmm...' Mimi was playing for time again. 'And what would the plans for Maskatchka show exactly?'

Jacob was at a loss. He looked around. Well they could start by re-building the devastated park – they could do with some comfortable benches in the sunshine where grown-ups could sit, and over there they could put a sports area where children could kick a ball around. The cosy houses and wooden cottages could be fixed up; the leaky roofs mended and old fences painted in rainbow colours. The unkempt lawns could be mowed and the old linden trees pruned, the church spire could once more be covered in gold and an up-to-the-minute school founded for dogs. A golden sandy beach could be created along the embankments of the Daugava River, all the holes could be filled in along the quiet streets and a swimming pool could be built in the big hole excavated at site Number 13.

Jacob really had come up with a plan it seemed. But the residents of Maskatchka – the dogs and freckle-faced Mimi – didn't make a sound. Jacob was starting to regret having spoken. Giving speeches wasn't his strong suit.

'That's the most ridiculous thing I ever heard,' Mimi said. The dogs agreed with her immediately, all quite convinced she was right. 'I would never have imagined that a Lame Duck like you could come up with something so … BRILLIANT!'

The dogs looked at each other in astonishment.

'After what we've just done to his limousine, Master Conman Skyscraper won't be expecting our plan to be something so simple. It's such a crazy idea that it will work perfectly – and then it won't be a crazy idea but a great one!'

It took some of the dogs a while to realise that the plan might actually work. The Boss growled, 'But it can never work anyway. Where are we going to lay our hands on maps of Free Maskatchka?'

'Please calm down. There's no need to worry,' Mimi told them, smiling broadly. 'Jacob here will help us!'

'Me?!'

'My cousin is great at drawing maps – when he

grows up, he is going to be a town planner like his dad. That is someone who prepares (and DRAWS) plans,' Mimi explained to the attentive dogs.

The dogs sighed in relief. So everything was decided! Jacob would start drawing the map of Free Maskatchka right away!

Conman Skyscraper, a spy and his bodyguard

The workmen had gone home to dinner with their families. The evening sun created long reddish shadows. Here and there grasshoppers chirped. House martins circled, slicing through the air with their sickle-like wings, their twitters loud in the silent park, before a flock of starlings passed over in a wave; flying tightly together like a ball, or breaking loose and spreading out. When darkness eventually fell and the first stars appeared like cracks in the blue bowl of the sky, some quiet activity could be observed in the far corner of the building site.

'Are you sure that I am *really* the best one to do it?' whispered a small boy, dressed in black from head to toe. His hands and face were being blackened using cinders fished out of Eagle's kitchen woodburner. They blended in so well with the darkness that it felt to Jacob like his own hands were drifting satellites, lost in the cosmos.

'Yes, Jacob,' responded one of the dogs, still in his prime but with a lame leg. 'We dogs are of no help here!'

'Exactly,' the girl insisted, her freckles faint in the starlight. 'You won't drool on the paper, you won't scrape the floor with your claws and you won't smell of dog. Plus, you are shorter than me and, all in all, quite easy not to notice. *Therefore* you are the most suitable candidate for this part of the operation!'

Jacob was so nervous that the newly drawn map of Free Maskatchka rustled in his hands like wrapping paper.

'Be as quiet as a mouse!' Mimi hissed as Jacob set off on tiptoe across the park towards the hut.

Sneaking up beneath the window, Jacob was able to hear someone yawning with exhaustion.

'The Maskatchka Liberation Plan must be

ya-wn-awesome but I will *work it out*! But before I do, I'm just going to have a *tiny* nap … five minutes should be enough…'

A moment later and the sound of loud hissing snores drifted out of the hut. Then the door opened and the bodyguard slipped quietly out. Jacob shrank back as far as he could – if you half-closed your eyes, you might not have seen him at all – he tried to breathe as soundlessly as possible, although he felt like his breathing was drowned out by the ground vibrating with every beat of his heart. His mouth was dry with fear but even a quiet swallow might be loud enough for the bodyguard to hear.

A match scratched and lit up the surroundings. Jacob smelt cigarette smoke. The bodyguard stretched and sighed. A tiny glowing light travelled upwards, smouldered there a moment then slid back down again. A quiet whining could be heard through the door of the hut.

'Stay strong, Bianca, we will save you!' Jacob thought.

The bodyguard whistled quietly and Bianca slid out of the hut. Her snow-white coat stood out in the darkness and, wagging her tail, she stuck

her wet nose into the bodyguard's big palm before the two of them moved slowly away from the hut. Bianca's jangling chain was taken off.

'Run! Run as fast as you can!' In his mind, Jacob screamed to Bianca despite knowing that even if he did call out to her the poor thing wouldn't understand a word that wasn't in Russian.

Jacob finally had the chance to slip into the hut. All he had to do was swap the plans for 'Skyscraper Forest' with those he had drawn for a Free Maskatchka. But it turned out this was easier said than done. Crumpled, smudged bits of papers covered in writing and scribbles lay scattered all over the place; untidy piles of bills lay on the floor, shelves and chairs... Where, in all this muddle, would he find the papers he was looking for? Heaps of charts, graphs, tables and numbers were piled on the bed where the terrible Master Conman Skyscraper lay fast asleep having his five-minute nap, his face deep in the pillows.

All of a sudden, Jacob's eyes were drawn to some neatly folded papers, standing out in the confusion, placed neatly on the bedside table. Grand Conman Skyscraper's plump little hand was lying on top of them, looking like a poisonous jellyfish. There was no doubt in Jacob's mind that these were the plans for Skyscraper Forest! Holding his breath, Jacob gently tugged at them, a centimetre at a time, until at last he had pulled them out. Now he just had to put his own plans in their place, but ... Jacob heard the bodyguard coming back! He had no choice but to throw caution to the winds. He lifted up Master Conman's hand, threw his plans beneath it, let the podgy mitt slam back down and made a mad dash for it.

Conman Skyscraper woke instantly and roared, 'GUA-A-A-ARDS!' but Jacob was already out of the door, dashing away. 'CATCH HIM!'

The bodyguard immediately set off after Jacob, who noticed that Bianca followed too – maybe this was her chance to make a run for it.

'Just wait til I get my hands on you!' the bodyguard called after him, breathlessly.

Bianca issued an order too, almost under her breath – 'Catch him!'

If Jacob hadn't been scared witless, he would have stopped in his tracks and double-checked:

'What did you say?'

Had he misheard? That wasn't Russian?!

'Look, he's tiny! All in black, too! Catch him Bianca, catch him!'

Bianca growled and, her instinct as a huntress burning within her like a flame, outran the bodyguard and almost drew alongside Jacob. So she *could* speak Latvian – her peppery Russian

accent gave her words a sharpness as if a pungent spice had been added.

'Dressed in black like a pirate!' the bodyguard panted. Jacob couldn't quite remember where he had heard his voice before.

The small boy ran faster than he ever had in his whole life. Thank goodness he had memorised the maze-like streets of Maskatchka, although the bodyguard seemed to know them like the back of his hand too as every so often he almost ran straight into his chest! Bianca, too, chased after

him with the energy of a wild beast on the scent of a forest hare!

Jacob ducked into an empty doorway, smelling strangely of abandoned shadows, while the bodyguard and Bianca went running past him. He could hear them calling out and barking to each other in the distance. But his escape was made all the more difficult by the strange party being held at the Academy of Dreamers, meaning that hordes of *City People* were wandering aimlessly through the streets of Maskatchka.

Some of them had sad, chalked faces painted on and moved slowly in a silent dance. To his horror, when they caught sight of Jacob, they stuck to him like shadows, copying his every move. The boy could hardly make his escape unnoticed with such a ridiculous group of followers! In the end, he had to twist and turn in a series of complicated moves so that the entourage, shadowing his every move, became a tangled knot of intertwined arms and legs.

Trying to avoid further entanglements with the party-goers, and peeping warily round every corner where the bodyguard and Bianca might be lurking, Jacob headed back to his friends in the secret hideout as fast as his legs would carry him.

He was starting to run out of puff when he spotted the bodyguard and Bianca, dangerously close again. How could he dodge them?! He was exhausted and almost ready to give himself up…

Suddenly, a tram came rumbling towards him, filling the length of Moscow Street with a warm glow. A wild idea sprang into his head. Could he *possibly* carry it off? Jacob had seen big boys in the city centre larking around doing just this, but he had never tried it himself. His dad didn't approve of this sort of thing and Jacob himself had never been keen on trying, either. But at the very moment the back of the tram sailed past him, Jacob leapt suddenly sideways – the bodyguard and Bianca stopped in their tracks, dumbfounded, searching about themselves for Jacob who seemed to have vanished into thin air. Then they noticed a small figure squatting like a frog on the small platform at the back of the tram – such a tiny perch that only a child could possibly fit on it – waving goodbye to them.

For a moment, Jacob's eyes met the bodyguard's. The boy shrank back in horror as he did a double take – were his eyes deceiving him? But the tram raced away, leaving his pursuers behind in the dark night.

Jacob's head was spinning. The tram tore through the darkness at the speed of an underground train – he felt as if he were flying through the Rockies. Jacob had been on the Metro in Paris and to Disneyland too, so he knew it was a good comparison. After a couple of stops, Jacob jumped off the tram and made a few detours through the streets of Maskatchka, just to make doubly sure that his pursuers would lose track of him and Bianca wouldn't pick up his scent.

He headed for the secret meeting place as arranged. It was a round, wooden church – once on a list for renovation but now doomed to oblivion.

When he got there the Boss got to his feet to greet Jacob properly, trying to hide the pain from his injured leg. The puppies wagged their tails with such delight that they almost stumbled onto their noses, but Mimi only grumped.

'Oh-my-God-what-a-bird-of-misfortune-you are! Nothing is simple when you are involved!'

'God has nothing to do with it. That's just me.' Jacob replied gravely.

'Did you do it?! Did you swap the plans over?!' Aunts, uncles, godfathers and cousins all crowded round to question him.

Jacob nodded nervously.

'Could I have a word in private please?' Jacob turned to Mimi and the Boss. 'Just the three of us.'

Disappointed, Zephyr and Sapphire cuddled up at the paws of one of their godmothers.

Jacob bit his lip without speaking.

'Spit it out then,' Mimi snarled impatiently.

Jacob felt very alone, only he knew exactly what

he had seen. He wanted to share it with his friends because he hoped that saying it out loud – something that seemed so immense and unsolvable – would make it shrink in size and become small and insignificant. Trembling with horror at the thought of what he had to say, the boy blurted out the painful truth.

'Boss, I heard Bianca speaking Latvian as clear as day … chasing after me paw for paw alongside the bodyguard! Bianca is the spy we were looking for!

'And Mimi, when I was on the tram I looked right at the bodyguard and there was no mistaking him, even in the dark. The keeper of Skyscraper Forest, the *personal bodyguard* of Master Conman Skyscraper is Eagle! Remember him saying he got the job as a bodyguard?'

He had said it now. His words bounced round the trio like an uneasy ping-pong ball. Unexpectedly, they didn't seem to provoke any sort of reaction at all until Mimi started laughing.

'Amazing!' she exclaimed. 'Why didn't I think of that before?!'

The Boss stared at the girl in shocked disbelief. Jacob, however, let out a sigh of relief. Now he knew that Mimi would take care of everything.

'I should have seen it sooner! It all started when he came to Maskatchka! Just look at him, trying to take me in like that, ha-ha!' Mimi turned to the Boss. 'He's trying to make our friends look bad to stop us looking at *him* too carefully! HE is the spy! JACOB BIRD is the real SPY!'

All the wishes in the world

The air in the round church smelled of rotten timber and centuries-old dust. If there had been any corners, darkness would have congealed there in thick clots. Instead, the darkness circled around itself, scraping lightly against the floor, letting out long deep sighs. Despite the warmth of the night, Jacob was trembling. He lay curled up on the builders' scaffolding, too scared to move in case he drew the attention of the evil monsters below, just waiting to gobble up all the miserable, unhappy little boys who had been abandoned by everyone. Jacob's only hope was that the monsters didn't like unhappy-tasting things and his great unhappiness might save him.

There was nothing he could do or say. No matter how Jacob tried to defend himself, Mimi and the Boss simply didn't believe his story. They walked out, leaving him on his own in the dark church, telling him never to show his face in Maskatchka ever again.

Jacob truly was a bird of misfortune. Was it someone else's fault that he was so miserable or his own? Now the boy was determined to feel like the most miserable person in the whole world! Awful Mimi didn't believe that he could drown Riga at the bottom of the river – but he'd only had to wish for it – and now Jacob wished for the whole of Maskatchka, Mimi included, to sink to the very bottom! That would show her!

The raging river in full flood! Jacob would ride the crest of a swelling wave like a horse, white foam on its bit, as it opened its mouth and swallowed Maskatchka... It would become a silent, soundless underwater world, its wooden houses like the wrecks of sunken ships, dogs swimming between them trying to catch passing fish, their fur like water weed, and Mimi's shouted orders would disperse as bubbles through the water, each one holding words like pearls in shells...

Jacob stopped. Nobody would survive such a catastrophe! Not even his dad on the other side of the city! And what would he have to say if he knew that Jacob had dreamt up another disaster rather than something nice? He could just imagine what Mimi would say: 'Oh-my-goodness-what-a-bird-of-misfortune-you-are, fancy making a wish like that! You have to wish for something that will help everybody!'

But if a wish was only good for everyone else and not for Jacob too, surely that wasn't fair either!

The boy hammered his fists against the wooden boards, feeling well and truly like the most miserable bird or boy in the whole wide world. But he discovered that feeling so miserable was also a bit exhausting and, really, there were other more important things to worry about, such as the sound of claws scraping against boards and the long, deep sighs of darkness wafting straight into his face. In the gloom of twilight, the figure of darkness awoke and took shape. Jacob trembled even more violently.

The boy took courage and called out, 'Who are you?!' But the figure of darkness remained gravely silent. 'WHAT DO YOU WANT?'

The harder he stared, the clearer the figure's outline became – two white eyes glowing in the darkness, a nose … no, a wet muzzle, grey fur, not a single tooth in his open mouth…

'GRANDDAD!' Jacob cried emotionally. At last, a familiar face … a familiar nose! 'Have you been left behind? Were you asleep? Did I wake you up?'

But Granddad just stared blindly into the darkness of his world and said nothing, sniffing the air and moving slowly towards Jacob on stiff, dragging legs. The boy helped the old dog to make himself comfortable by his side.

Jacob felt himself going red. What if Granddad had heard what he had said about the catastrophe? Was he wondering if he had been wrong to let the nasty little boy in to Maskatchka? The only answer Granddad gave was to blow a heavy puff of smelly dog's breath in Jacob's face.

Jacob would have to wait until morning to make his way back to normality – a soft mattress on his bed, silence yawning lazily in the corners of the room and the same old view of roaring cars and busy people outside the dining-room window… He had memorised the way back to his own home, he told Granddad.

Jacob slowly untied the ropes connecting his thoughts to his dream version of Maskatchka, carefully drawn up for 'Operation Free Maskatchka'. He was almost ready to set these thoughts afloat on the river like a beautiful wooden sailing ship, anchored since forever on the banks of the Daugava River; the golden cupolas of its church for sails and the fences of its mansions as the sides of the ship. Eagle, being a sailor, would stand at the helm, steering the ship out to sea – Mimi, the Boss, his team and the puppies would all be on board … he would never see any of them ever again…

From now on, Jacob would only be able to read about a special breed of talking dogs in the secret section of the Register of Endangered Species.

'Specially protected breed of talking dogs.

The most gifted specimens mastered the skills of human language while living alongside humans in their dwellings, from where they were later evicted.

The breed selected the territory of Maskatchka as its natural habitat.

The breed is now extinct due to humans' selfish lifestyle choices and irresponsible construction strategies.'

Jacob felt himself becoming increasingly alert. An idea formed in his head like an egg and, perched on the tip of his tongue, it was almost ready to hatch.

'Protected breed!' he exulted. 'Granddad, we are saved! YOU are saved and the whole of Maskatchka with you! We can save Maskatchka – I promise you! From all the wishes in the world, I choose one and one alone – I wish for a free Maskatchka!' The boy hugged the elderly dog, burrowing his face into his grey fur as if it were a soft, downy comfort blanket.

The gold cupola sails billowed proudly once more, hoisted high above the deck of the sailing ship that was Maskatchka.

Footsteps and muffled voices could be heard through the half-open, heavy oak church door. Someone spat neatly, blue and red lights started dancing like whirly witches inside the church. A voice from the police car called out: 'Here they are! The Toughnut brothers! Let's get them!' This was followed by the sound of hurried footsteps and the blaring sirens and glaring headlights disappeared.

Morning slid into the church through the half-open door.

Jacob's tummy rumbled.

He was hungry.

He wished he had eaten something! If only this one, *last* wish would come true then his only wish would be for Maskatchka to be free again, he wouldn't wish for anything more!

Jacob's eyes were itchy after his sleepless night but he trailed after blind Granddad and his infallible sense of smell in search of food, although there was nothing that his friend found in the city's bins that the boy fancied eating for breakfast.

On the lawn under the bridge lay two bearded men, snoring soundly. Jacob would not have given them a second glance if it weren't for the partly eaten loaf of bread and empty bottle lying in front of their noses. Jacob's tummy ached with emptiness. He crept quietly over to them. What harm could there be in borrowing a tiny bit of bread? They wouldn't even notice! Nothing terrible would happen if he borrowed another piece. Just a little bit more … bread had never tasted so good … the more he ate, the hungrier he felt. He had already polished off half the loaf when Granddad howled in pain as a massive boot landed a kick in his side and an enormous hand grabbed Jacob firmly.

'What are you up to, you thieving monkey!' roared one of the bearded men. He snatched the loaf away from Jacob. 'You're not safe anywhere these days, not even on your own turf, with any old mutt allowed across the border! You remember that! The Maskatchka bins are ours!'

Jacob was so frightened he could do nothing but howl, 'I'm soooo hungry...'

'Not my problem,' the bearded guy muttered, shoving the boy away. 'I was going to make that loaf last a week! Lucky for you, you're so small it's not worth grinding your bones to make flour for another loaf!' the man sneered.

A week?! Grind his bones for flour! Jacob ran, and Granddad followed as fast as he could!

What a horrible thought. There were people who lived for a whole week with the same terrible hunger pains that Jacob had felt that morning for the first time in his life! Granddad moved his tail meaningfully, maybe saying 'I agree'. But then again, maybe not...

Jacob thought about it all carefully. He decided to change his mind again – his final wish to benefit everyone should be food for all. But seeing as his second-to-last wish had already been granted, Jacob thought he would have to switch them around and somehow return the bread he had just eaten. He could not get his head around how that could be done and even if it could, it would also mean that at least one person in the world, namely Jacob himself, would still go hungry...

His head spinning with these thoughts, Jacob's legs carried him forwards and, like a dog following a scent, they took him straight to the heart of all the goings-on in Maskacthka. All paths led him back to the park.

A specially protected breed of dog

The workmen stood by the dilapidated fence, shaking the new plans in their hands. Some of them had already set to work following the instructions and were eagerly painting the fence poles in all the colours of the rainbow while another group of workmen, stripped to the waist – their backs as tanned as dark crusts of rye bread in the sun – were busy mending the wooden houses' leaking roofs. Others lazed around on the white-painted verandas or lay under apple trees, their hats pulled down over their eyes, sometimes waving towards the hired diggers, concrete mixers and cranes which they now had no idea what to do with.

There was no park to speak of anymore. There were no trees left, no canopies of leaves with the cool breath of shadows playing beneath them. Now, rays of sunshine streamed in all directions from the park into the surrounding streets, like broad rivers of light. Conman Skyscraper's prefab hut had once been encircled by trees like silent guards but with the trees all gone the enemy's hidey-hole now sat in full view as if on the palm of an empty hand.

After a sleepless night, Jacob's senses were swimming in waters of fearlessness. No icebergs shaped like Skyscraper Forest were able to sink his Maskatchka sailing ship. Tucking a secret message behind Granddad's old, worn collar, the boy sent the elderly dog to fetch the pack of talking dogs. Jacob, all alone, made for the glaring light of the park.

Bianca the spy, still ruffled from sleep, was the first to sneak out of the prefab, the jangling chain dragging behind her as heavily as the promise she had given to the enemy. After stretching out her stiff limbs for ages, she tried to make herself comfortable – looking about for a clean spot before disconsolately settling down in the dust. Her teary eyes wandered over the desert that had been the park. There was nothing to look at; she ran her eyes from north to south, from east to west – nothing. Then, she was blinded for a moment by dozens of tiny black specks whirling in front of her before they fused into a black figure – right there, on the edge of the park.

'Woof!' Bianca warned. 'Woof, woof, woof!'

It was really very handy that watch dogs did not need to speak any particular language, to warn their masters of intruders.

The bodyguard, dressed in black as always, rushed out of the hut. He looked like a foreigner in his dark sunglasses but Jacob recognised him immediately, sailor's pipe between his teeth and arms crossed over his chest. As he approached, he scorched the ground at Jacob's feet with his glare, even with his dark sunglasses on.

'Hey, Titch! Scam! Get lost!' the bodyguard called. Then he looked again. 'It's the tiny intruder! He's back!'

Finding himself suddenly in the bodyguard's

vice-like grip, Jacob couldn't help a couple of unwelcome tears. The bodyguard was shocked – he had heard crying like that somewhere before!

'JACOB?! I had no idea it was you – your face is so smudged and dirty! I took you for someone else...' he added suspiciously.

After all the amazing happenings of the long night, Jacob had totally forgotten that his face was covered in black gunk; he probably wouldn't even have recognised himself in the mirror!

'What are you doing here so early in the morning? Out walking the paths of the moonstruck? When I was at sea I would often see other sailors roaming the ship's galleys at midnight as if wandering through the maze of their own dreams.' Removing his sunglasses to reveal his calm, weather-beaten, familiar face, Eagle winked one razor-sharp eye at Jacob.

As if reading some invisible notes, Bianca was sniffing round the little boy, suspicious and wary.

Jacob immediately blurted out, 'Eagle, I need to speak to the owner of Skyscraper Forest straight away! It's of the utmost importance!'

Eagle shook his head.

'No way, Jacob. I've been given my orders – it's out of the question. You see, my job is to stop anyone getting close to him. Is it a matter of life and death?' Eagle asked this as if he thought it highly unlikely any reason Jacob gave would come anywhere close to being *that* important – he was just too small.

'When those big diggers have squashed all the wooden houses of Maskatchka to pulp it will be too late,' Jacob replied.

Jacob only hoped that the people living in the houses had woken up early enough to get their bags ready and set off in a long stream, carrying their belongings with them.

'When the dogcatchers show up, ready to chase all the talking dogs out of Maskatchka and into cages at the dog pound, there'll be no chance left to save Maskatchka…'

At this, Bianca froze. Eagle rubbed his tired eyes as he heard the boy speak like that, as if to make sure his eyes and not his ears were deceiving him.

'What a terrible picture you've painted for yourself!' Eagle shrugged, chasing away some annoying thought and trying not to look at the scene of desolation that had been the park.

Eagle continued joking, 'And what talking dogs are to be found in the vast expanse of ocean which is your imagination?' Bianca started fidgeting, then yelping in horror.

Jacob tried to speak as slowly and loudly as he could so that all he had to say truly got through to the bulky man's ears, and in the right order, too. He had played "Chinese whispers" before so knew how important it was to speak clearly if you had an important message to get across. He also knew how important it was to make sure your wishes were heard clearly and not blown about by the winds.

'Specially – Protected – Breed – of talking – dogs – which – should – be – listed – in – the secret –

sections – of the Register – in which – a secret decree – issued by – very important people – states that – a reserve – must be – established – in Maskatchka – where – the Talking – Dogs – could – live – in their natural habitat – and the species – would be – protected – from extinction.' Jacob took a breath. 'All – all – further – CONSTRUCTION – on the plot – would be forbidden.'

Before Eagle had time to open his mouth, Bianca suddenly shouted, 'And we would all be saved!!!' her eyelashes quivering nervously.

The world came to a standstill, the globe stopped spinning and birds froze in flight like paper decorations hanging in the sky. Eagle spat on the ground and rubbed his eyes in disbelief. Even when he was at sea, staring at the horizon for months on end, his eyesight had never deceived him. But now he was seeing things! A talking dog! It must be all the stress he was under – yes, definitely – the new job, the night-time chase and a sleepless night – it must be stress doing something funny to his senses!

Knowing her secret was out, Bianca hid her muzzle in the sandy ground for a moment, only to lift it out again and start pacing restlessly, yelping, 'Is it true? Is it true that the dogs of Maskatchka could be protected?! Are talking dogs so special?' Bianca's eyes were gleaming; Jacob noticed a silent star of hope alight in the depths of her intense dark eyes. Her warm red tongue licked Jacob's hand while she whispered excitedly, searching carefully for the right words in Latvian, 'What a silly dreamer I've been! I dreamt of finally finding myself a proper home with a place to sleep in the hallway, between the shoes and the doormat, my own food bowl and a big, warm hand that would stroke my head in the evening... What is a dog for, after all, without an owner and a house to guard?!

'When that smart limousine appeared in Maskatchka, I followed it in the hope that maybe I would find an owner of my own. As the days went by, I thought more and more about finding a home and an owner. I even managed, in secret, to learn a few words of Latvian so I could understand orders! How happy and proud I was when the door of the limousine opened and I was allowed to hop in and drive off with my new owner!

'My dreams fell apart straightaway ... I showed my new master the most hidden corners of Maskatchka and kept away anyone who wanted to hurt him but I never received a single kind word or the smallest stroke ... I was treated like a prisoner, tethered to this heavy, ugly chain!' The snow-white dog turned her eyes away in disgust. 'Not to mention all this...' she said sadly, looking at the desecrated park. 'My own paws have had their part to play in the destruction of Maskatchka, and I never realised before that its streets have been my only true home! The Boss, our puppies and the pack were the only ones who ever really loved me… And now what will happen to them all? Oh, what have I done…'

Eagle was scratching his bald head. As a sailor, he had seen it all – mysterious pirates staring at his ship as if seeing a whale of steel. Strange creatures of the deep, never mentioned in schoolbooks, that swam ashore on the desolate beaches of faraway lands, showing great yellow teeth strong enough to crack open even a whale of steel. But never, never had he heard animals speak in the language of humans!

They were suddenly interrupted by a sarcastically venomous voice behind them. 'Let's not waste time with this SENTI-METAL nonsense.'

It was Mimi, of course, her hands pressed tightly against her sides, her eyes scanning the trio sharply. Behind her, the Boss was looking at his mate, his eyes full of hurt. With him were the puppies and the whole army of talking dogs, their chests, which raised proudly in battle, now sagged as they took in the bewildering meaning of the trio's conversation.

'First of all,' Mimi spat, 'licking Jacob's hand as

if she were as pure as snow may be very touching but if Bianca truly regrets her actions, she will have to prove it.

'Secondly, I sincerely hope that everyone else here regrets their actions just as deeply.' Here, Mimi turned to Eagle, but her eyes could climb no further than his rock-hard chest. 'Couldn't you find another job, Eagle? Being a bodyguard is so *un-sensical*. Why would you guard people and their possessions when they are not even yours? It's a bit dog in the mangerish, wanting to look after something that's not yours – totally *ridickly-less*!'

Mimi dug into the dirt with her toe and scanned the dusty park, her lips pursed in silence. Then she threw Jacob a look in which he thought he saw a touch of guilt – was she apologising?

'Thirdly…' Jacob rushed to remind her, knowing that there had to be a 'thirdly' for the first two points to count.

'Thirdly, Granddad was left to spy on you. Spying on a spy, get it? You never imagined that a lame, blind, old (retired) dog would be sent to snoop, did you?!' Mimi gloated, very pleased with her clever idea. 'In the morning, Granddad came back with two messages. He spent a very long time giving us the first message. There was a lot of tail-wagging and nose-twitching, but he told us that you had a plan and it was not the scheming plot of a spy. As the dogs trust Granddad's *instinctions* (or whatever you call them) completely, we must, or rather I must, apologise for not believing you,' Mimi gulped. Out of the corner of her eye she glanced at Eagle in his bodyguard's uniform, and Bianca the spy, the very picture of snowy-white innocence. 'The second message we found tucked behind Granddad's collar.'

Mimi extracted the secret missive from between

Zephyr and Sapphire's teeth, each holding a corner as they sat quivering by the Boss's right paw. It was the stolen map of Skyscraper Forest, across which the following had been scrawled:

WARNING!
CONSTRUCTION WORKS TO CEASE
IMMEDIATELY AND THE SITE USED AS A
SPECIAL PROTECTED RESERVE FOR US
(TALKING DOGS ARE MORE PERSUASIVE
THAN ANY HARD FACTS)

'What does this mean?' Mimi frowned.

Jacob insisted that the most persuasive argument had to be the existence of talking dogs – far better than any horrible plans they might cook up in an attempt to save Maskatchka! Grand Conman Skyscraper would not guess that plan, not in a million years!

Mimi studied the dogs uncertainly. Finally understanding how important they were, the dogs coughed in embarrassment, cleared their throats and tidied up their fur. In actual fact, they looked a very scruffy bunch and not a group to be taken very seriously. However, it must be said that if their powers of speech had left Eagle – who had seen the most amazing landscapes and the most terrible creatures in the world – lost for words then maybe something really could come out of it.

And then as if to showcase their advanced language skills, the dogs started loudly debating the whole thing.

The tiny skyscraper

'Wow! Maskatchka is far more exciting than all the sea pirate raids put together!' Eagle whistled, observing the motley crew of dogs – godfathers, godmothers, uncles, aunts, cousins and the Boss; their ears all pricked up as they discussed in businesslike, hushed tones what future action was required to carry out the plan. Bianca was desperately upset because her family and loved ones hadn't spoken to her yet, after her confession. She still had to earn back the pack's trust.

Bianca and Eagle, who had the map of Skyscraper Forest and the secret message in his hand, were about to disappear into the dark interior of the prefab again when Mimi called out, 'Don't let the ship sink, Eagle!'

Everyone waited, holding their breath and listening hard. They could hear Eagle talking, then he was reading out loud the message on the map of Skyscraper Forest.

'What is the meaning of this?!' they heard Grand Conman Skyscraper screaming in fury. His voice was so shrill it could cut crystal, very different from Eagle's humble tones. 'They are MY maps!!!' and 'What do THEY want?' as well as 'Barking mad! Talking dogs!! What do YOU TAKE ME FOR?!'

Jacob, Mimi, the Boss and his dogs all listened, ears pricked. If everything went according to plan, they should now hear Bianca speaking clearly in Latvian – but they didn't hear a thing. The Boss was scratching around impatiently in the sand, growling to himself. Mimi was doing the same. It was not until the first dog of Maskatchka sneezed loudly, shrugging in disappointment from his muzzle to the tip of his tail, that a quiet whining gradually becoming louder, emerged from the hut.

'Good morning, Master! Did you have a good night? I hope you slept well. My name is Bianca

'... in case you ever wondered. It may not be that important but, maybe, you would like to call me something? Dog owners usually do when they have a new pet – although I never expected to be your *pet* as such – but I did hope for a pat on the head every once in a while...'

'What is she doing?! That isn't part of the plan!' Mimi hissed. The Boss gave a short bark in agreement.

Hearing his bark, Bianca came to her senses and started chanting in a sweet, almost sing-song voice the speech she had practised so carefully:

'I am Bianca, a Siberian Laika – a dog of noble origin from faraway Russia. I ask you to listen to my message. In recent years I have lived in Maskatchka with the other dogs. We are no ordinary canines, Master – as you now realise, we are talking dogs. We are many in number yet not enough to protect the breed should it come under threat. If our habitat is destroyed, the entire species of talking dogs will become extinct. We wouldn't have minded living our lives underground, keeping our gift secret. But now your actions, Master, have forced us to take extreme measures. If Maskatchka is destroyed, we will demand the city council

establish a reserve for our breed of specially protected talking dogs. You must see, Master, that should we go ahead with this, hordes of animal welfare activists, scientists, zoologists and enviromentalists all around the world will campaign for our protection and lobby against the destruction of such a protected, unique breed's natural habitat. All current and future construction work will be halted. Master, please understand that there is no point investing in this project. I trust … I trust that I have been a faithful servant to you, Master,' Bianca added in conclusion.

The Boss sighed in relief – Bianca had got it right! All of a sudden, a figure shot out of the door like a canon ball, a chubby finger pointing back into the darkness of the hut as he shouted, 'VENTRILOQUISTS! You will not deceive me! I've seen plenty of circus performers like you!' The rotund figure spun on his heel and turned to face the Maskatchka freedom fighters, who stood frozen to the spot in fear.

Mimi looked at him and started to say something.

'But you're…'

She gasped in disbelief, then giggled. Her giggles got louder and louder until they spilled over into laughter, roaring and rushing like a river until Mimi found the strength to say what was blatantly obvious yet so very hard to believe.

'...A CHILD!'

The small but chubby figure stared at the weird-looking girl and pack of dogs. He wore glasses on the tip of his nose and his mouth was pursed into a heart shape. He was wearing grown-up clothes – a smart suit and a tie, his hair combed over neatly with a straight parting.

'So what? Do you think you're so grown up?!' growled Master Conman Skyscraper, who was actually a little boy!

'And to think I believed that Master Conman Skyscraper was some sort of terrifying monster!' Mimi sniggered.

'WHAT?' shrieked the chubby boy, his glasses skewiff on his nose. 'Master Con-what!!!'

'Master Conman Skyscraper!' the girl repeated. 'Or as you would have it, Grand Master Skyler Scraper, get it?' She laughed with glee at her own joke. 'But maybe Master Piescraper would suit you better!'

The stout little boy went red. He clenched his plump hands into fists and squeaked breathlessly.

'I might be a child but I am completely different from all other children! I don't have time for your circus tricks so please, send these clowns away!' He pointed to Eagle and Bianca. 'I don't want play with other kids or any sort of mutt – so get lost! I don't have time to waste with your childish games, playing vets, dog schools or kennels.

I'm building the *future,* don't you see? And I have a schedule to respect. I have to do it now, as soon as possible! Do any of you, for example, have a *business plan*? How are you going to pay for your education? Do you have pension plans for your retirement? How are you going to reduce unemployment? What kind of furniture are you going to demand for your home?'

Mimi, scowling, said nothing. Most probably, she had never thought about such things. Neither had Jacob. They were the sort of things that just happened, like being given your breakfast, dinner and tea. Eagle spat on the ground, looking as if he had already given too much thought to such things. You probably had time to think about such things and many others, out at sea for months.

'The streets of Maskatchka are our furniture!' the Boss of Maskatchka replied in militant tones. 'The paving slabs are our bathroom tiles...'

'The soft lawns of Maskatchka's parks are our beds,' one of the uncles rushed to add.

'Our orchards are our spacious, well-equipped kitchens,' joined in one of the godfathers.

'Not to mention the alleys that are our hallways,' chimed in some of the aunts.

Master Conman Skyscraper stared at the talking dogs with growing alarm. As they praised the wonderful comforts Maskatchka offered them at every turn, they were showing exactly how amazing their power with words really was. But he seemed less alarmed by the dogs' miraculous speaking abilities than by the prospect of his plans falling through just because of a few talented mutts.

'Talking dogs are more persuasive than any hard facts,' he read and, at a total loss for words, put his head in his hands. 'As if we didn't have enough with restrictions over sand dune areas, coastal zones and river towing sections, we now have to contend with an urban national park area that we can't lay a finger on! Do you not see that your ghastly plan will have the most horrendous *consequences*? I had it all worked out – have you no idea of the *financial loss* it will bring to the economy?' The boy in his smart suit then went on to list a series of complicated notions, all sounding like terrifying beasts even to Eagle's ears. Man-eating 'infrastructures' and 'resources' roared in the darkness, harsh 'factors' and winged, fire-spitting 'inflation', not to mention the ulcer-provoking, exotic dragon of 'credit'. The Maskatchka freedom fighters found themselves floundering in a dense jungle of unknown terminology, with nothing to hand to fight back.

Once again, the boy straightened his glasses,

which had the habit of slipping down to the end of his nose, and summed up by saying:

'My project would fail completely, just because of a handful of scruffy, runaway performing dogs and a few old shacks! What a loss! And no *compensation*! My father will be most displeased about this! He was more proud of me and this project than any idea I have ever had before! Quite honestly, he usually doesn't even remember he has a son at all – once, he and dear Mamma forgot all about me and I was left at school. That was when they decided I desperately needed a chauffeur-driven limousine and bodyguard... My father is responsible for very important affairs of state, you see. Thank goodness my bank account isn't overdrawn!' the boy whined, twiddling his fingers and studying the group of Maskatchka freedom fighters.

'Maybe we could simply put all this behind us? I'll give you the cash to buy a new hovel to live in!'

The dogs were shocked, indignant even. What use did they have for the scraps of paper and bits of metal that people called money? They would not dishonour themselves by giving up their territory without a fight – they decided they would challenge him to a duel! But instead, Mimi threatened him with reinforcements again – in the shape of green campaigners and animal rights activists. She could see that Master Scraper looked as if he knew all too well what that could mean for his plans.

By now, Scraper seemed to be getting really agitated. He glared at the Maskatchka freedom fighters through the slits of his eyes.

'Is there no way of getting round this situation without suffering financial loss?' He seemed to be talking to himself. 'Is there some way I can still make a *profit* out of these circumstances? How can I best exploit the situation to my own advantage?'

BUSINESS PLAN

TALKING DOGS → ? → PROFIT

The small, rather bewildered Maskatchka freedom fighters now bobbed along on a tide of strange words, numbers, bank notes, coins, tables and diagrams. Only one of them had any experience of navigating foreign waters.

'I believe there is an opportunity here for us to work together,' Eagle pronounced, rubbing his hands together. His eyes resolutely scanned the horizon where they made out an inviting, sunburnt edge. 'Speaking as a sailor, a man who has seen the world, I must say that I have never come across an inner-city nature reserve – it would be the first and only one of its sort, a one-of-a-kind reserve for the talking dogs of Maskatchka! Grand Master Skyler Scraper will be acknowledged the world over as the saviour of this rare breed, which he rescued from extinction by saving and protecting its natural habitat. On our part, we shall undertake not to harm the good name of Grand Master Skyler Scraper by mentioning the damage done so far, but rather promote the name he has made for himself from such an early age, resulting in further success and, no doubt, the generation of *profit*.' Eagle winked at the number-crunching whizz kid. 'It's in our *mutual interest*,' Eagle added, temptingly.

The boy squinted thoughtfully at Eagle. Behind his narrowed eyes he seemed to be weighing up the pros and cons of his proposition.

Finally he announced: 'Such an outcome would result in higher profits than the total losses suffered in the event of the project being cancelled.'

The dogs of Maskatchka looked at each other – in modern jungle-talk, did that mean they had done a deal?

Maskatchka was SAVED!

An overwhelmed Bianca wagged her tail high in the air like a white flag signalling a truce. The Boss, who had been longing to lick his mate's snow-white ear all this time, dashed over to his beloved and almost licked her to death.

But one person didn't seem to want to join in with the jubilations.

'So is that it? No fight, no struggle, no pursuit? Is it that simple? Not even some good old settling of scores or an argument to hammer out the details?' Mimi was indignant.

Scraper pulled out a pocket calculator and said, 'Calculating the difference between shared losses and investment of further resources, I conclude that any additional time *devoted* to settling

differences will *not pay off*. And now I must take
my leave and return to school. All other details
will be discussed at the board meeting.'

Mimi thought it better to keep quiet, seeing as
she had nothing witty or, more to the point,
sensible to say in response. Grudgingly, she had to
admit that Jacob Bird's plan had really been more
than just a tiny bit successful. Probably quite a lot
more, in fact.

High time for the bird of misfortune to feel happy

The sky was so blue that the earth's colours sparkled before your eyes, and warm beams of sunshine hummed like moths through the streets of Maskatchka. It was a perfect day for fishing on the riverbank.

Eagle, puffing on his sailor's pipe, sighed in satisfaction as he pulled up the occasional enormous bream or perch. Mimi, standing nearby up to her knees in the Daugava so she could get as close as possible to "those underwater non-animals (because fish are *not* animals)", hissed every so often as she caught a tiny minnow.

'What do you want with those great big old fish when you can feast on delicious, tiny little ones?' the naughty girl said in her defence, storing away another weeny fish in her blue plastic bucket.

The reeds swished quietly, a busy insect buzzing through them now and then. The sun climbed up and down the conker-shaped bumps of Jacob's spine leaving freckled trails across his shoulders. Jacob would never forget these last few summer days – they had been so incredible and colourful!

Lying on the riverbank with the puppies sleeping sweetly beside him, barking and chasing after a couple of Maskatchka cats in their dreams, Jacob was tracing the outlines of a new map in the sand. On the left, he had drawn the five-storey building on Brīvības Street, on the right the low wooden house where Mimi and Eagle lived. Now both of these were Jacob's homes.

A voice suddenly called out from the Maskatchka house side, despite belonging to the tall building on Brīvības Street.

'Oh, there you are! I knew I would find you lazing about by the river on a day as beautiful as this!' the voice said.

DAD?! Dad was here at long last!

He had returned from whatever far-flung place he had been to, bringing with him not only lemonade for the children but tobacco for Eagle, too. Now he was here, his absence seemed to trail off behind him – endless yet at the same time unexpectedly short.

The grown-ups shook hands and exchanged a few words then, looking happy to be back together, clapped each other on the shoulders. Eagle started to tell Dad about the changes which were afoot in

their district and Dad had to sit down as he listened to how Jacob's plan had saved Maskatchka.

When Eagle had finished his story, Dad nudged Jacob with his shoulder. 'And we thought it was the end of the world! But look how many good things have come out of it for both of us! And we are not the only ones to have done well!'

Then Dad told them all about the huge problems he had had with his business, which had been on the brink of bankruptcy. How he'd had to say goodbye to Jacob's tutor as well as Marta, their housekeeper, as he simply couldn't afford to pay their wages. He told them how their landlady, Mrs Schmidt, was not prepared to wait any longer for the overdue rent and was about to turn them out onto the street. That was why he had left Jacob with Eagle and Mimi. But NOW, thanks to a *miraculous windfall, an unexpected deal* and *a lucky outcome* – Dad had come to take Jacob straight back home with him, but ... but why wasn't Jacob excited about that?!

Zephyr and Sapphire woke up at the sound of Jacob's sobs and started licking his wet cheeks in sympathy while the boy snuggled up with his little friends. He knew he would be incredibly sad to leave his new friends, even though he had wished desperately to go back home ever since first arriving at his uncle's house. Now his wait was over.

'Oh, I see!' His dad grinned mischievously. 'I think our four-room flat is big enough to house two extra guests!' He stroked the puppies with his big palm then hugged Jacob tightly. The boy sank into his father's arms and the smell of black coffee, the tang of metal coins, soap and – home! Jacob picked up a trace of that smell which, in the blink of an eye, transported him back to the other end of the city and he found himself in two places and two homes at the same time.

Jacob was almost the happiest boy alive. His happiness, like Riga itself, seemed perfectly complete...

But what would happen to the wonderful, golden sailing ship of Maskatchka, left to its own devices without Jacob at the helm?

Following all that had happened in the park, builders, carpenters and workmen streamed into Maskatchka and proceeded, quite happily and purposefully, to carry out the necessary works to ensure that the area was indeed the ideal natural habitat for talking dogs. In response to the dogs' requirements, they replanted trees and marked off certain fence posts to serve as dog telephone poles. The tumbledown wooden houses waited bashfully, shielded by the veil of apple-tree branches, for their miraculous makeovers. Dotted around the area, fixed in the most conspicuous spots, were bright, hard-not-to-notice signs featuring the investor's logo, something which Scraper explained to anyone not already aware of the fact.

Seeing that Eagle's house was right at the entrance to the reserve, he had the task of guarding the entry. When he realised this he had rubbed his hands in satisfaction. Since the sensational news about the miraculous dogs was still to spread *Beyond*, he wasn't very busy as yet. However, he was all geared up to welcome the expected onslaught of excited visitors who would need to be warned against feeding the dogs with treats and lemonade, criss-crossing their usual routes, disturbing them whilst on the rounds of their natural, wild, urban habitat or trying to force them to speak.

Bianca was promised her own special spot between the slippers and doormat in Eagle and Mimi's hallway and was well on the way to becoming the favourite dog with the visitors they had had so far. Bright-eyed and affectionate, she would beg for strokes and kind words and accept gifts from adoring admirers (such as gold collars, crystal food bowls and goose-down pillows, she said!) pose happily for photos and play joyfully with visitors' children. After their visit, so many children would cry for days on end for their own pet, that soon the cages of the city dog pound were empty. Meanwhile, the Boss would watch over his patch from the roofs of Maskatchka, his bushy eyebrows blown flat to his head in the wind. Only the occasional lucky visitor would catch sight of him, although everyone claimed to feel him breathing down their necks wherever they went in the reserve. Granddad, lying by the gates of Maskatchka, would treat them to one of his penetrating gazes. His looks could see what sighted eyes were unable to detect, letting visitors know that nothing here would be like it was the world beyond – they only had to open their eyes and believe, he seemed to say, and the story would never die but continue living on the streets of Maskatchka forever.

'You can take the puppies for a walk every day,' Dad said. 'And when they grow up, they will take you for a walk, and all four of us will visit Eagle and Mimi and the other dogs. Maskatchka is not going to disappear because, just like Riga, Maskatchka will never be ready!'

Reinis Pētersons is an award-winning professional illustrator, animation, film and visual artist who lives and works in Riga. His many awards for film and children's illustrations include the Latvian Artist of The Year Special Prize, and he has been nominated for international prizes including the Astrid Lindgren Memorial Award, and the IBBY Hans Christian Andersen Award.

Žanete Vēvere Pasqualini was born in Riga. She graduated in Foreign Languages from the University of Latvia in 1995 and took a course in Italian language and culture at the University of Perugia. She was the first consul in Italy after independence and divides her time between Latvia and Italy. She has been a literary agent for Latvia since 2015. In addition to *Dog Town* Žanete has also translated the following into English: children's poetry collection *The Noisy Classroom* by Ieva Flamingo (Emma Press); novel *The Green Crow* (Peter Owen Press); short stories 'The Birds of Ķīpsala Island' by Dace Rukšāne and 'The Shakes' by Svens Kuzmins (*The Book of Riga*, Comma Press) and short story 'The Quarry' by Jana Egle (Words Without Borders).

More great books from *Firefly Press*

 Alex Sparrow and the Really Big Stink, by Jennifer Killick. Alex is a secret agent in training and a human lie-detector. Summer Reading Challenge selection. £6.99

 Aubrey and the Terrible Yoot by Horatio Clare. When Aubrey's father falls under the spell of the Terrible Yoot, Aubrey sets out to break it. Winner of the Branford Boase Award 2016. £7.99

 The Jewelled Jaguar by Sharon Tregenza. Is the fabulous Aztec knife dividing Griff's family really cursed? £6.99

 Gaslight by Eloise Williams. 'A darkly delicious romp through the backstreets of Victorian Cardiff,' Emma Carroll. £6.99

 Scrambled by Huw Davies. When a new headteacher starts at his school, Davidde is unfairly labelled a troublemaker. But then he discovers scrambling! £6.99

order now from:
http://www.fireflypress.co.uk

Firefly